It's too late to back out now. . . .

"What's wrong with you guys?" I asked. "Just yester-day we were all complaining that we hadn't had a job in eons."

"Sure, I could use the money," Allie agreed. "But a party for Jennifer? It's going to be a disaster."

"It'll be a total flop." Julie nodded grimly.

ROSIE'S POPULARITY PLAN

by Carrie Austen

SPLASH™

A BERKLEY / SPLASH BOOK

THE PARTY LINE #4: ROSIE'S POPULARITY PLAN is an original publication of The Berkley Publishing Group. This work has never appeared before in book form.

A Berkley Book/published by arrangement with General Licensing Company, Inc.

PRINTING HISTORY
Berkley edition/July 1990

A GLC BOOK

Splash and *The Party Line* are trademarks of General Licensing Company, Inc.
Cover logo and design by James A. Lebbad.
Cover painting by Mike Wimmer.

ISBN: 0-425-12169-0
RL: 4.8

A BERKLEY BOOK ® TM 757,375
Berkley Books are published by The Berkley Publishing Group, 200 Madison Avenue, New York, New York 10016.
The name "BERKLEY" and the "B" logo are trademarks belonging to Berkley Publishing Corporation.

PRINTED IN THE UNITED STATES OF AMERICA

10 9 8 7 6 5 4 3 2 1

ROSIE'S POPULARITY PLAN

One

"You won't believe what she's done now!" Becky and Allie complained to Julie the second she got on the school bus that morning.

It had been weeks since our last party, and we'd all been moaning about our empty wallets. I had thought a new job would have been good news, and so I had told them about it as soon as I got on the bus. But they weren't very happy about it. And I wasn't very happy about *that*.

"What's the terrible news?" Julie asked.

"What makes you think it's terrible news?" I asked.

Julie nodded toward Becky and Allie, who had been making perfectly horrible faces behind my back. "Well, if Becky's tone of voice isn't enough of a clue, check out her face." Becky took advantage of the attention to screw her face into an even more contorted grimace. "I ask you," Julie went on, "is that the face of a happy girl?"

"The news is even worse than Becky's face," Allie put in.

"Oh, wow," Julie joked. "What could be worse than that? Don't tell me—let me guess."

She looked around the bus while she thought. The Ryan twins were throwing spitballs at each other in the back of the bus. Of course, most of them were landing on the kids around them, which was completely disgusting to everyone except the Ryans, who thought it was hilarious. Julie watched them for a few seconds, then wrinkled her nose.

"I know. She said we'd do a party for the Ryan twins," she guessed.

"Worse."

Julie pursed her lips. "*Worse?* Rosie Torres has done something worse than that? Rosie, my best friend, the girl I've known since kindergarten, the sensitive artist who wouldn't hurt a fly? I don't believe it!"

"She got us stuck doing a party for Jennifer Peterson!" Allie and Becky hissed at Julie.

"The Jennifer Peterson who's new in our class?"

"Who else?" Becky asked, rolling her eyes.

"I just hoped there might be another Jennifer Peterson," Julie said with a sigh.

"I wish there were," Allie groaned.

"What's wrong with you guys?" I asked them. "Just yesterday we were complaining that we hadn't had a job in eons. I thought we all could use the money."

"Sure, I could use the money," Allie agreed. "But a party for Jennifer? It's going to be a disaster."

"It'll be a total flop." Julie nodded grimly.

I couldn't believe my friends were all acting that way. I had thought that since Julie Berger is my very best friend, at least she would have stuck up for me. But she was just as negative as everyone else.

"That's not true," I said, a little hotly. "Besides, you thought the party for Casey Wyatt was going to be a big flop, but it wasn't! What makes you think this will be any different?"

"Oh, get real, Rosie," Becky said. "At least Casey has friends."

"Yeah," Julie said. "Who are we even going to get to come to this party?"

Right then the bus pulled into the school driveway. It was just as well, because I figured I'd need to think about the whole thing some more. I had to have some answers ready for the next time we all talked.

Before I could say anything about meeting at lunch, though, Allie spoke up. "Let's talk about this after school, okay? Maybe we can all walk home together and have a mobile meeting."

I felt relieved. At least Allie was being sensible about this. But that's Allison Gray for you—she's always so practical.

"I mean," she went on, "I don't want to spoil my lunch having to talk about Jennifer and this awful mess we're in."

* * *

Usually I think The Party Line, the party business I run with my three best friends, is the most terrific thing ever. We have lots of fun, and we make lots of extra money. But there are times when this business seems like more trouble than it's worth. Right then was one of those times.

When we first started the business, it seemed like such a good idea. We'd filled in for a sick clown at Allie's littlest brother's fourth birthday party, and we'd gotten such great reviews from our pint-sized guests that another parent hired us right away to do a party for her six-year-old daughter. The rest, as they say, is history.

Allie got that first fateful phone call, but it was Becky Bartlett who got the brilliant idea of turning the phone call into a regular business. That's why Becky is president of The Party Line and Allie is vice president. I get straight As in math, so I'm the treasurer. Julie is the secretary, because she has the best handwriting. (But mostly what she does at meetings is doodle and pig out on the potato chips— or anything else that's edible. She still manages to stay skinny, though, which we all think is very unfair.)

We usually do about two parties a month, and we definitely like having the extra money. And we all like children, so doing parties for little kids is fun for us. Almost all our business is young children between four and seven years old. We'd only done one party for someone our age, and that was for Casey

Wyatt, who is absolutely the most obnoxious boy in seventh grade. It was really an accident that we ended up doing it at all, but it had still been a great party.

I didn't think it was so terrible to agree to give Jennifer Peterson a special thirteenth birthday party. In fact, I didn't think Jennifer was so terrible, either.

Jennifer's family had just moved to Canfield from Minnesota, and she'd entered Canfield Middle School in the middle of the year. If it were me, I wouldn't be able to decide which was worse: leaving all my friends to move to a whole different section of the country, or having to start making friends all over again in a school like Canfield, where practically everyone had grown up together. I knew Jennifer felt really shut out.

The way I knew was that I'd been paired with Jennifer for an English project a few days earlier. I hadn't wanted to be her partner, but I didn't have any choice. Our project was to interpret a favorite story in a new and different way, and I had to go to Jennifer's house after school one day to work on it. I had been dreading it, though.

My mom drove me to the Petersons' house that afternoon, and when she turned the car into Douglas Estates and pulled to a stop in front of a white two-story house with slate-blue shutters, I groaned to myself. *It figures snobby Jennifer Peterson would live in one of the fanciest parts of town,* I thought grimly.

When I didn't make a move to get out of the car, Mom asked, "This *is* twelve-ninety-six, isn't it?"

As if anyone could miss those enormous brass numbers over the garage door, I said to myself. Out loud, I said, "Yes."

"It looks like your partner is waiting for you," my mother said. Then I noticed Jennifer standing in the big front window, waving to me. For a snooty, stuck-up new girl, she sure was acting friendly.

"Just call when you want me to pick you up," my mom said, which was kind of a signal for me to get out of the car. I grabbed my backpack and hopped out.

Before I even got to the front door, it opened. Jennifer held the screen door open and gave me a big smile. "Hi," she said. "Come on in."

I could hardly believe it was really Jennifer Peterson. Was this the same girl who always sat by herself at lunch, as if none of us were good enough to share a table with her? Who never smiled? She certainly looked like the person whose first words in her new school were, "I moved here from Rock Valley, Minnesota and . . . and I hate it here!" (That was after our homeroom teacher introduced her and asked her to tell the class a little bit about herself.)

I tried to smile back as I moved past her into the hall. As she shut the door I looked around. Mail and newspapers were stacked on a pretty little table next to the door, and there was a big oak-framed mirror on the wall. I could smell something wonderful cooking in the kitchen. On the inside, Jennifer's house looked just like my dream house. Suddenly it wasn't so hard to smile.

Jennifer pointed toward the living room. It was painted robin's egg blue with shiny white trim. It had a big stone fireplace, framed on either side by tall built-in bookshelves painted the same dazzling white as the trim. On the floor was a big, soft-looking Oriental rug, sort of like the one I always use in Becky's attic but much, much nicer.

When Jennifer said, "We can work in here," I was thrilled.

"Really?" I squeaked. In my house, the living room is definitely off-limits for friends. It always looks beautiful, but it's certainly not for anything so ordinary as doing your homework. Don't get me wrong—I love my parents, and I love my home. Still, I always swore to myself that when I had my own house, I'd have a great big living room decorated as cozily as Jennifer's, and I'd use it all the time.

"Sure. Drop your jacket on one of the loveseats."

Jennifer had left a notebook and pens on the coffee table. If that ever happened in my house, you can bet my mom would have a lot to say about it.

I had just settled in when a tall blond woman came into the room. I thought to myself, *Uh-oh, this is it. We're about to get kicked out.*

But instead of yelling, she looked right at me and said, "You must be Rosie. I'm Jennifer's mother." Then she put out her hand just like I was another grownup and while we shook hands, she said, "It's nice to meet you, Rosie."

"Uh, thanks," I said. "It's nice to meet you, too."

"Well, I know you two have a lot to do," Mrs. Peterson went on, "but don't forget there are cookies in the kitchen when you're ready to take a break." She smiled warmly at both of us and left the room.

"Have you thought of a story we could use for our project?" Jennifer asked when her mother had gone.

I leaned back against the couch cushion and nudged my shoes off, following Jennifer's lead. I felt incredibly comfortable. "I kind of like 'The Ransom of Red Chief.' It's about this boy and some kidnappers—"

"I know," Jennifer interrupted. "It's one of my favorites. I love funny stories."

"Me, too." I grinned in spite of myself.

"But do you have any ideas about how we can use it for the project?" Jennifer asked.

Just then a huge, hairy dog trotted into the room and tried to climb into Jennifer's lap. I come from a tropical fish family; I didn't want to admit it, but such a gigantic dog made me a little nervous. Jennifer must have figured that out, because she shoved him away. "Down, Bear. We'll play later." Bear ambled out of the room, and she looked at me seriously. "Forget Bear, he won't bother you," she promised me.

I relaxed again. But I still wondered why Jennifer was being so nice when she acted so snobby in school.

"Do you want to rewrite the story as a play?" she asked.

I pondered the idea. It sounded interesting, but it would have taken too much time. I told Jennifer that, and then I added, "I thought I'd illustrate a scene from the story."

"You can draw?" Jennifer sounded impressed.

"Yes." Actually, I loved to draw. I never went anywhere without my pens and pencils and a small sketch pad. My friends always teased me about it. But then, Jennifer wasn't exactly a friend of mine. I didn't know what she liked to do, either.

"I like to write poetry," she told me.

The perfect idea popped into my head. "A poster!"

Jennifer and I mulled it over. We decided that I'd illustrate the story, and Jennifer would write a funny poem to go with it.

"It's not the kind of poetry I usually write," she said. "But I think I can do it."

"This must be a record," I said, checking my watch. I had been at the Peterson house only half an hour and already we had our project all figured out.

"You don't have to leave right away, do you?" Jennifer asked. She seemed kind of wistful. Suddenly I remembered something Mrs. Peterson had said.

"No," I answered, "but I think it may be time for a break."

Jennifer looked a little puzzled for a second, then

she brightened. "Right. Cookies in the kitchen," she said. "Follow me."

The kitchen was a big room at the back of the house. It had one wall all made of brick, with a real fireplace built into it. Mrs. Peterson was sitting at the big wooden table, reading a book.

"Oh, hi," she said, "I was just doing a little homework of my own."

I must have looked surprised, because Jennifer said, "My mom's taking classes at Taylor College."

"I've finally decided to get my graduate degree in art history," Mrs. Peterson told me. She said it casually, but I could tell she was proud of it.

"Are all those great art books in the living room yours?" I burst out. I'd been noticing what a great collection they had while Jennifer and I were getting our project together. My fingers had been itching to get hold of some of the beautiful books I saw on the shelves.

"Yes," Mrs. Peterson said. "But I bet you didn't come in here to discuss my library. Can I interest you in some homemade cookies?"

"What kind?" Jennifer asked.

I didn't care. In my house, cookies came out of packages from the grocery store. *Any* kind of homemade cookies sounded great to me.

"Oatmeal and chocolate chip."

Jennifer giggled. "She puts chocolate chips in everything." That was when I decided I liked the Petersons.

I liked them even more when Mrs. Peterson said, "Why don't you take a plate into the living room? Rosie, you could look at my art books if you'd like."

If I'd like! While I loaded a plate with cookies, Jennifer poured two glasses of milk. She arranged everything on a big tray that we brought out to the living room with us.

I pulled a big book about the artist Salvador Dali off the shelves and began flipping through it while I munched some cookies. They were still warm, and they were delicious!

I was trying to make some sense of a painting in which a bunch of clocks and watches appeared to have melted over tree branches when Jennifer started talking.

"It must be nice for you, growing up here and knowing everybody and everything," she said. Her voice was a little husky. "I know I made a big mistake on my first day when I said I hated it here, but I miss my old school. And all my friends."

"The kids at Canfield are pretty nice once you get to know them," I told her. *At least,* I thought, *most of them are.*

"*If* you can get to know them," Jennifer said. "It's hard to fit in when all the kids at Canfield have grown up together. It's like trying to crash a party you haven't been invited to."

I'd never really considered what Jennifer might have thought of us. What if we all seemed just as snobby to her as she did to us? One thing was for sure: since I'd been in her house, Jennifer hadn't once acted snooty or stuck-up. Maybe she was just lonely and didn't know how to make friends. I'd certainly miss Julie and Becky and Allie if my parents moved to another state. Still . . .

"Why did you say you hated Canfield?" I asked.

"Give me a break," Jennifer said. "It was my first day. I'd hardly slept the night before because we had just moved in and my room was such a mess. When I finally dragged myself out of bed and got dressed for school, my little brother spilled his chocolate milk all over my skirt at the breakfast table. I got lost on the way to school, so I was really late. And while I was at the office getting directions to the classroom, Casey Wyatt, whom I didn't even know at the time, made fun of my bookbag!"

It did sound pretty rotten. No wonder Jennifer blew up when she had to cap a crummy morning by standing in front of the class and talking about herself. She had a lot of spunk, actually. If it had been me, I probably would have burst into tears. I didn't know what to say to her. "What bookbag?" I asked.

"I don't use it anymore!" Jennifer said. "How was I supposed to know that all the kids in Canfield use backpacks?"

When I thought about it, the idea that we all used backpacks just because everyone else used backpacks was really pretty stupid. Jennifer realized it, too, and we both started laughing at the same time.

"I see what you mean," I said when we'd stopped

rolling around on the rug. "And you probably didn't know that no one at Canfield wears purple on Thursdays," I joked.

Jennifer almost lost it again. Then she got serious. "Really. I'm tired of not understanding jokes about things that happened last year—or maybe back in first grade! It just makes me feel even more left out."

I guess we were all guilty of leaving Jennifer out of things. All I could say was, "I'm sorry."

"Hey! I didn't mean you." Jennifer's blue eyes clouded, and she looked worried that she had offended me.

Mrs. Peterson walked into the room just then. "I thought you might need reinforcements," she said. She was holding a plate piled high with more cookies.

Once Jennifer and I had finally broken the ice between us, I started to have a really good time. We talked about all sorts of things—boys and clothes, mostly. And somehow I also ended up telling Jennifer about The Party Line.

"Phone call for you, Rosie," my mother said later that night.

"Hello?" I said, picking up the receiver.

"Hi, Rosie. It's Mrs. Peterson, Jennifer's mother."

I couldn't imagine why she was calling me. "Did I leave something at your house?" I asked.

"No." Mrs. Peterson laughed. "This is a business call."

"Business?" I suddenly realized that I probably sounded as if I'd left my *brain* at the Peterson's.

"Party Line business," she said. "Jennifer has a birthday in two and a half weeks, and I want you to plan a party for her. I know it hasn't been easy for her, moving to a new place in the middle of the school year, and I wanted to do something special for her. I had thought about throwing a party for her, but I didn't even know who to invite. Then she told me about your business, and it sounded like the answer to my prayers."

Once I'd realized how lonely Jennifer was, I wanted to do something nice for her, too. And I knew we could all use the money. The Party Line hadn't had a job in weeks.

"Sure," I said. We agreed that I'd give Mrs. Peterson a call and let her know what sort of ideas we came up with. It was pretty late already and I had homework to do, so I figured I'd tell everyone about it on the bus the next day.

How was I supposed to know it would turn me into as much of an outcast as Jennifer had been all those weeks?

Two

At lunch I was slow getting to the table I always
shared with Julie, Becky, and Allie. There was a
hole in my apple and I went back to the food line to
trade it in for another. Maybe that sounds silly, but
I wanted to be sure I wouldn't be sharing my fruit
with a worm.

When I sat down I saw Becky staring at Jennifer
Peterson. Jennifer was sitting by herself at a table
in the farthest corner, reading a book. It was true
that Jennifer had done that every day since she'd
started at Canfield, but now that I knew her a little
better I felt kind of bad about it. Still, if no one even
wanted to talk about Jennifer's party at lunch, I sure
couldn't invite her to sit with us.

"Can you believe the bio assignment?" Julie said
when I sat down at my regular place. "Like I don't
have enough studying to do lately!"

Julie was studying for her bat mitzvah, a special
ceremony that Jewish girls have when they're
twelve or thirteen. She'd told us about it, and we all
knew how busy she'd been. The rest of us had been

kind of busy ourselves—we'd decided to plan a special surprise party to help Julie celebrate.

"It's not just studying, either. I have so much other stuff to do before my bat mitzvah ceremony," Julie went on.

"Oh, Julie, quit complaining," Becky said with a big grin. "All you did for months was tell us how great it was going to be and now that it's finally happening all you do is gripe. Aren't you forgetting some important fringe benefits we should be hearing about?"

Julie blushed. "Did I tell you about the gorgeous dress Goldie sent me?"

Now this was really interesting. Goldie was Julie's grandmother. She lived in Florida and was always sending Julie terrific presents.

"Julie! Goldie sent you a dress and you didn't even tell me!" Of the four of us, Julie and I were the most into clothes and fashion. I felt a little hurt. Becky obviously knew about the dress, and Julie hadn't said a word to me!

"Relax, Rosie. I just got the dress yesterday. I haven't told anybody about it yet!"

Becky winked at me.

"How did *you* know about it?" I asked her.

"Hey," Becky said. "I'm a very helpful person. As we were walking in here Julie dropped her notebook. And while I was helping her pick up the hundred million little pieces of paper that fell out, I saw a card that said, 'For my darling granddaughter to wear at her bat mitzvah. Knock 'em dead, Julie. Love, Goldie.' "

Julie's blush, which was already intense, deepened as Becky recited Goldie's message from memory.

"So tell us about the dress, Julie," Allie said. Allie sometimes stammers when she gets flustered, so she has a lot of sympathy for people in embarrassing situations. It was just like thoughtful Allie to help Julie out. And as Becky's extra-special best friend, Allie usually knows how to distract Becky when she starts teasing.

"Well, it's really sophisticated," Julie said. "It's bright pink with silver beads at the neck and cuffs. The sleeves are kind of sheer. They're made of some kind of gauzy material that has sparkles in it."

"Ooh," I breathed. "I know that dress! I saw it in *Saucy*. It has a big pink satin ribbon around the waist, right?"

"That's it!" Julie seemed so excited. Who wouldn't be? Goldie had given her the very best dress in the entire world to wear on her special day.

"Gee, it sounds really grown-up," Allie said, a little wistfully. Allie is the youngest—and still the shortest—of all of us. She has a hard time finding more grown-up fashions that fit her.

"Of course it's very grown-up." Becky got a gleam in her brown eyes. "You're going to be a woman soon!" Julie had told us that the bat mitzvah ceremony celebrates a girl's entry into adulthood. Officially, it meant that Julie would then be responsible for herself, although as she pointed out, it was really only symbolic. She wasn't about to go get her own apartment or anything!

"Tell that to my mother," Julie said. "She almost wasn't going to let me keep the dress. She thought it was *too* grown-up!"

"Oh, no," I cried.

"She changed her mind," Julie said. "Heather and Laurel really helped convince her."

"Really?" Allie asked. To the rest of us, Julie's two older sisters Heather and Laurel were mostly famous for bugging Julie to get off the phone so they could talk to their boyfriends for hours at a time.

"I could hardly believe it myself," Julie laughed. "Now that I'm going to be bat mitzvahed, everyone in my family is getting a little sentimental. My mom actually said, 'My little baby's growing up.' "

Becky pretended to stick her fingers down her throat and Julie giggled.

"That *is* kind of hokey," I admitted. "But I think it's really nice, too."

My friends all looked to me. "You would!" they shouted. They tease me a lot about being a hopeless romantic.

"So, what are you doing this week that makes you so busy?" Becky asked. It was important that we find out what Julie was up to so we could get together to plan her surprise party. Until Becky had come up with the party idea, I had never realized how inseparable the four of us are. Every time we'd tried to talk about our party plans, Julie seemed to appear out of thin air.

Julie began to count off her obligations on her fingers. "Today and tomorrow afternoon I have to practice my Torah reading for the ceremony. Then one night my mom and I are going shopping for shoes to match the dress—hopefully we can find them in one trip." Julie stopped for breath. "Goldie hasn't decided yet what day she's flying up from Florida, but whenever she arrives we'll all be going to the airport to meet her."

Allie cleared her throat and began doodling with her pen on her lunch napkin. That was a signal.

"Then there's homework. It's going to take at least one whole night to do the bio project," Julie went on. "Just what I always wanted to do—chart the dominant genes of six generations of fruit flies!"

"I think it's kind of interesting," Allie said. (Allie likes to be organized, and really gets into projects like that.) She began scribbling a tiny little note on her napkin. Then she glanced across the room and sighed. "Isn't he gorgeous?"

"Who?" Julie nearly jumped out of her chair.

Allie pushed the napkin across the table to me. On it she had written, "Tomorrow afternoon right after school."

I had to keep Julie distracted so I could pass the note to Becky. I clasped my hands over my heart as if I were in total shock. "Allison Gray is interested in a *boy*? Who is he?"

Allie bit her lip and stared at a table in the corner. Then she whispered, "Dylan Matthews."

Julie strained to get a better look at dark-haired Dylan. As I shoved the note toward Becky, I had to admit Allie had found a great way to divert Julie's attention. Just mention a cute guy and Julie and I both go a little weird. Becky and Allie—especially Becky!—tease us a lot about being boy-crazy. And Dylan Matthews *was* one of the cutest guys in the seventh grade.

Still, the look on Allie's face confused me a little. She was staring at Dylan like someone suffering from a genuine crush. And Allie's not a super actress. Was Dylan just a way to distract Julie, or was Allie finally starting to notice the opposite sex?

By the time Julie turned back to us, we'd all seen the note and silently agreed to meet and begin our top-secret party plans.

Lunch was nearly over.

"Meeting after school, right?" Julie asked.

"Right," I said.

"So I guess it's finally time to talk about our disaster party," Julie commented as soon as we were outside school. The four of us were walking home together instead of taking the bus. With the Ryan twins on our bus it was nearly impossible to have a business meeting on the ride home. Besides, we needed privacy for this particular meeting.

"I wish you'd stop saying that, Julie!" I snapped.

"What's with you?" Becky asked. "She's just saying what we all think, anyway."

"That's just it," I said. "Why are you all so convinced we can't give a good party for Jennifer?"

"Rosie." It was Allie. "Jennifer is not exactly popular. In fact, I don't think she has *any* friends at all. And I don't think she even wants to make friends. You heard her say she hates Canfield."

"Even if we could find people to come to the party, what kind of fun can we have with Jennifer there?" Becky asked.

"Maybe she doesn't know how to have fun," Julie said. "I've never heard her laugh, or even seen her smile."

I was afraid to tell them some of the things Jennifer and I had talked about the day before. Even though Jennifer hadn't made me promise to keep our talk a secret, I'd have felt like a traitor, telling my friends about her innermost feelings.

"I think she's just lonely," I finally said. "Anyway, I already told Mrs. Peterson we'd do it."

"How did you end up getting this job, anyway?" Becky demanded. "Oh, wait. I know!"

"You and Jennifer are partners on that English assignment Ms. Lombardi gave us," Allie finished.

"So, did she come over to your house or something?" Becky wanted to know.

I told them about going to the Petersons' and about somehow ending up telling Jennifer about The Party Line. "She told her mother, and . . ."

"Now we're stuck," Julie sighed.

"A job is a job," Allie said without enthusiasm.

"What kind of party could we do for her?" wondered Becky.

I was glad my friends were acting like professionals. We walked along in silence for a few minutes.

I felt a little guilty. I hadn't exactly defended Jennifer, and it wasn't just because I didn't want to tell secrets. I was also a little afraid that my friends would think I was a jerk if I told them how nice Jennifer seemed to me. Either way I felt like I was doing something wrong, and it really bothered me.

"I just don't know enough about Jennifer to have any ideas," Julie said after a while.

"Except we know she doesn't have any friends and she doesn't like living here," Becky reminded her.

"Maybe if she got to know some kids a little better she wouldn't hate it so much," Allie ventured.

"That's it!" I said excitedly. "We'll have a 'Welcome to Canfield' party!"

My friends looked puzzled.

We were almost home and I needed to work on this new idea of mine a little more. "I think I know how we can do it," I said. "Now that we agree that we have to do the party, just give me a few more days to work this out. Let's talk again at our regular meeting this Sunday in Becky's attic, okay?"

"Okay," my friends agreed. *Whew!* I thought. *Things are finally going right for a change!*

Three

"Thank goodness Julie's busy today!" Allie said the next day after school as we settled on a bench at Van Fleet Park. It was time for our secret party planning meeting.

"She'd die if she knew we were getting together without her!" Becky said.

"Not if she knew why we were meeting," I told them. Julie was going to love being the center of attention at her surprise party.

Even though it was Becky's idea to have the party in the first place, we were going to have it at my house. After all, Julie is my extra-special best friend. And since we'd decided to make the party a sleepover, it made more sense anyway, because I don't have any brothers or sisters to get in the way. My mom had already said it was okay, too.

"The party's a week from Friday, right?" Allie asked.

"Right," I said.

"When is Jennifer's party?" Becky wanted to know.

With a sinking feeling, I realized I'd agreed to do Jennifer's party on Saturday, the very next day. That was going to make things tricky for us. "Uh . . ." I said.

"I knew it!" Becky pounced. "Jennifer's party is supposed to be the same day, isn't it?"

"Not quite," I said timidly. "It's the next day."

Becky groaned.

"That's okay," Allie said comfortingly. "We can do both. We'll just have to get everything planned ahead of time, that's all."

I shot her a grateful look.

"Well, we better start planning, then," Becky said. "Any ideas?"

"I thought since Julie's bat mitzvah ceremony celebrates her becoming a woman, we could make that the theme of our party," I said.

"I like it!" Allie said.

"We could start with a glamorous dinner party," Becky said, getting into it. "If it's okay with your mom, that is."

"My mom said we could have the run of the house all night," I said. Becky and Allie both gave me envious glances.

"It must be great being an only child," Becky mused.

"Believe me," I said, "you'd miss your brothers and sisters if they weren't around." It was funny how I secretly wished I had brothers and sisters, but my friends who did were always complaining about them.

"I wouldn't miss David at a sleepover!" Becky insisted stoutly.

"Maybe not at a sleepover," I agreed.

"You could never have a glamorous dinner party at my house," Allie said. There were five kids in Allie's family, and sometimes the Gray house seemed like a cross between a zoo and Grand Central Station.

"I have some great recipes I've been dying to try out," Becky said. Becky's parents own the Moondance Café, which occupies the ground floor of the big old Victorian house they live in. Because she works at the Moondance after school sometimes, Becky is sort of our food expert, and so she usually handles that end of our party plans. But sometimes Becky's idea of a great recipe is a little strange.

"Becky, I don't know how to break this to you," Allie said seriously, "but raisin-potato salad and green whipped cream are out of the question," she finished, and burst out laughing.

Becky had actually put raisins in the potato salad at the Moondance one time last year when her parents had let her help out in the kitchen. Her most notorious stunt, though, had taken place one St. Patrick's Day, when she "decorated" the cream that was meant for the apple tarts.

"You guys have no imagination," Becky sniffed.

"Seriously, Becky," I said, "what sort of food did you have in mind?"

"Well, chicken Kiev isn't that hard to make," Becky said, mollified. "And neither is rice pilaf."

"It sounds very sophisticated," Allie said.

"I can make green beans with almond slivers," I volunteered.

We decided we'd buy all the ingredients and make the whole dinner at my house. Our plan was for Julie's mom to drop her off at my house around six o'clock that Friday night. Julie would think she was coming over to watch a movie.

Usually when we rented movies, we'd watch at either my house or Julie's house. But wherever we were, we always had pizza and popcorn. So Julie wouldn't have had dinner when she arrived that night. We were going to rent her favorite movie from the video store, anyway. Why not do it all?

"We'll eat by candlelight," Allie said.

"And we can use the good china," I added.

"This will be our best party ever," Becky said. Just then she looked up from the pad she was scribbling our menu on. "Uh-oh," she muttered, "here comes our worst party nightmare."

Jennifer was walking Bear along the park path. They were heading straight toward us.

"Check out that sweater," Becky said. "I bet it glows in the dark!"

"Shh." Allie looked worried. "She might hear you."

Sure enough, Jennifer and Bear were walking more slowly as they got nearer. I found myself dreading the possibility that she might stop and talk.

Bear sniffed at the grass beside the park bench. Jennifer let him explore as far as his leash would stretch while she looked at us. Finally, she said, "Hi, Rosie."

My friends watched out of the corners of their eyes. I tried to ignore them. "Hi, Jennifer. How's Bear today?" The dog stopped sniffing when he heard his name and looked up at me, wagging his tail. I could have sworn he was smiling. Maybe he hadn't made many new friends yet either.

"He's still a dog," Jennifer said, giggling. Naming a dog after another animal *is* kind of funny, even if he was almost as huge as a bear. I started laughing, too.

Next to me, Becky and Allie rolled their eyes. They weren't even smiling.

"Hi, Jennifer," Becky said pointedly.

"Hi," Allie nodded to her.

It was obvious they were insulted because Jennifer hadn't said hello to them. I felt very awkward, and didn't know what to say. I had to get Jennifer away from my friends. "Could I walk with you and Bear for a while?"

"You want to?" Jennifer sounded stunned. "I thought you didn't like dogs."

"In general they make me a little nervous, but

Bear's nice. Besides, he's on a leash." I wasn't convinced Jennifer was surprised only because of the
dog. I didn't think she'd expected me to leave my
friends to join her.

"I'll make sure he behaves," she promised.

"I'll be right back, guys," I said quickly to Becky
and Allie.

As Jennifer and I rambled down the path, I tried
not to think about what my friends were probably
saying. Instead, I studied Jennifer's sweater. It was
knitted from thick red yarn and covered with bright
green and blue bows. It *was* kind of bright, but it
was also really pretty.

"Is that a hand-knit sweater?" I asked her. "I've
never seen one like it before." It was true. Cinderella, the boutique my mother owned, carried some
pretty exotic clothes, but Jennifer's sweater was
unique.

Jennifer grinned and pushed her long blond hair
out of her face. "My grandmother made it for me."

There must have been more than a hundred bows
on the sweater. "I bet it took her forever!" I said.

"She loves to knit."

"It really brings out the blue in your eyes," I said.

Jennifer glowed with pleasure. "Thanks!"

"You know, that sweater would look great with
skinny black leggings," I said. I couldn't help it—
I'm always trying to redesign people's outfits. My
friends never mind, because they're used to my

"makeover madness" by now, but suddenly I worried that Jennifer would think I was insulting her.

"I mean, it looks great with those corduroys," I said lamely. "I just like to fool around with clothes and stuff."

"It's okay, Rosie," Jennifer said. "I really like the way you put your outfits together. I wish I could look as great as you do."

"You always look nice," I protested.

"Not like you. I never would have thought to twist a colored scarf and use it as a belt, like you did last week."

"That was just something I copied from a fashion magazine," I said.

"But you're good at it," Jennifer said. "I'm not."

"I could show you how to do it, too," I offered. It wasn't until Jennifer's eyes lit up that I realized just how anxious she was to have friends to do things with.

"Really?"

"Sure. We have to get together to finish our 'Ransom of Red Chief' project anyway. We could do it then if you like."

"Great."

"I'll call you later," I said, "and we can figure out what day to do it. It should be soon, though, because our assignment's due next Tuesday."

Jennifer looked so happy that I felt really happy, too. I looked across the park to where Becky and

Allie sat waiting. Jennifer followed my glance and said, "You should probably go back, huh?"

"I guess so," I said. That reminded me—I wanted to say something to Jennifer about why Becky and Allie had acted so cold, but I didn't know how to do it. Was there a nice way of telling Jennifer that she'd been rude?

"Your friends don't like me very much, do they?" Jennifer asked, not looking at me.

"I think they think you're a little stand-offish," I said frankly.

"Why would they think that?" Jennifer seemed honestly confused.

"Well, I think they felt weird that you said hello to me but not to them," I blurted out.

"I know." Jennifer sighed. "I just felt so funny. I mean, I don't know them very well and they were staring at me like . . . like I had green hair or something. I guess I was afraid to say hello to them. I'm sorry. I guess I made it hard on you, didn't I?"

I understood how Jennifer felt. I thought she was wrong not to say hi, but I thought Allie and Becky were wrong to behave as they did, too. "It's all right," I said. "I'll call you tonight, okay?"

I could feel Becky and Allie's eyes on me as I walked back.

"Sorry I was gone so long," I said. I wanted to explain to my friends why Jennifer seemed so snobby, but I didn't know how to bring it up.

"That's okay," said Allie.

"We were just worried about you, that's all," Becky said.

"Worried?" I repeated. I didn't know what Becky was talking about.

"Yeah, we were worried that you'd hurt your eyes looking at that sweater!" Becky said, snickering.

"I think it's a nice sweater," I said. "Maybe it doesn't look that great with those corduroys, but it's actually pretty cool."

"Rosie, only you could see the fashion potential in a sweater like that," Allie said.

Right then I decided to give Jennifer a makeover—the best makeover I'd ever done. I'd start with her clothes. Jennifer had a lot of great stuff, but I had to admit she was right about one thing: she sure wasn't good at creating interesting combinations. Most of the time she looked okay, but a little on the dull side. And when she did wear something bright and fun, like that outrageous bowed sweater, she made it look out of place and a little ridiculous by matching it with something boring and ordinary, like those corduroy pants.

Jennifer was really pretty, too. She had a perfect oval face with wonderful high cheekbones. With her crystal-blue eyes, creamy skin, and long blond hair, she could look like a model if she'd just give herself a chance. Maybe if my friends saw a better-looking Jennifer on the outside, they'd realize that she was just as nice on the inside, too.

"Earth to Rosie, come in please." Becky was

speaking through cupped hands directly into my ear. I realized I'd been staring off into space.

"Sorry, guys," I kidded them, "I was communicating with my spaceship. Did I miss anything interesting?"

"Shall we get back to business?" Becky asked. We didn't call her Madame President for nothing. You could always count on Becky to remind everyone what needed to get done—even when it wasn't an official Party Line job.

"What else do we need to talk about for Julie's surprise party?" Allie asked.

"How about theme presents?" Becky said.

"That's a brilliant idea," I said. "You mean, like get her a sexy nightgown or something?"

"Rosie!" Allie looked shocked.

"Well, you know what I mean," I said. "Something a little more, uh, womanly than a long t-shirt."

"Why don't we go to the mall tomorrow after school?" Becky asked. "Is that okay with everyone?"

"What's Julie doing tomorrow?" I wanted to know.

It was Allie's job to keep track of Julie's schedule. She pulled out a little notebook and flipped through it. "Tomorrow could be a problem," she said. "What if that's the day Julie goes shopping with her mother?"

"Oh, wouldn't it be awful if we ran into her at the mall?" Becky shuddered.

"We could probably hide whatever it was we were

buying for her," I said. "But she'd never forgive us for going out without her."

"Or she'd figure out we were up to something, and start playing detective," Allie said. For a while Julie had been planning to be a detective, and she is actually still pretty good at it. (Julie changes her mind the way most people change their clothes. A few months ago she had wanted to be a professional baseball player, but now she wants to be the first person to land on Mars.)

"What about the day after tomorrow?" I asked.

"She should be working on her bio project," Allie said.

"But she'll probably be watching television," said Becky.

"What are we going to do?" I yelled in exasperation.

"I know," Allie said. "I'll call Mrs. Berger. If she says they're shopping tomorrow night, we'll go the day after tomorrow."

I knew how much Allie hated to call people's parents. She had to do it all the time because of Party Line business, but sometimes it made her nervous and she got a little tongue-tied.

"That's okay, Allie," I offered. "I have to call her anyway to go over all the details of getting Julie to my house. I'll find out and let you know." Of course, that was assuming I could find the twenty seconds that evening when Julie's older sisters wouldn't be on the phone!

Four

"Time's up, class. Pass your tests forward," Ms. Lombardi said. We were in English class, where we'd just gotten a nasty surprise: a pop quiz.

Jennifer had a stack of books on the corner of her desk. When the boy in front of her reached back for the quiz papers, he bumped into the stack. Everyone in the room jumped when the books crashed to the floor.

Jennifer leaped out of her seat to collect the scattered books. Trying to do it quickly, she muttered something that sounded like "oof dah."

"Woof da!" Casey Wyatt screamed with delight. "Woof! Woof! It's a Jennifer dog!"

Jennifer scrambled up from the floor, her face bright red. But she stood up straight and looked Casey right in the eye. Very firmly, she said, "I did not say *woof*. What I said was *uff da*. U-F-F D-A."

She didn't bother to explain what *uff da* meant. I guessed it was something people in Minnesota said when they were upset.

Casey quieted down, and I leaned back in my chair

and sighed. Until then, I hadn't realized I was tense. But now that I knew how uncomfortable Jennifer felt in school, it really bothered me to see Casey pick on her.

I'd called her the night before, and she was going to come to my house around four o'clock to work on our project. She couldn't make it right after school because her mother had a class and Jennifer had to keep an eye on her little brother, who was only seven. I made a mental note to ask her what *uff da* meant.

Ms. Lombardi read a short story out loud to us after the quiz. I paid attention, but my eyes kept straying toward Jennifer. If I'd been publicly insulted like that, I'd still be steaming.

Jennifer seemed completely absorbed by the story, though. She had a rapt look on her face, and was obviously hearing things in the words that I was missing. But then, she was a poet. I preferred colors and shapes to words, but Jennifer was just the opposite.

When the story ended, Ms. Lombardi closed the book and looked around the room. "That was an atmospheric piece," she explained. "That means it was trying to create a *feeling*. What feeling did you get from it? Jennifer?"

Jennifer smiled. She looked up at Ms. Lombardi and said, "It was magic."

Everyone in the room cracked up. Jennifer had no way of knowing that that was a really old joke in school. Because of all the noise in the room, I couldn't possibly have explained it to her unless I'd gotten up, walked over, and shouted in her ear. And from the look on Ms. Lombardi's face, that was not a good idea.

Way back in fifth grade, we'd been studying pollution in Ms. Anderson's class. We were trying to find out whether some of the chemicals manufacturers put in household cleaners are really necessary.

Ms. Anderson had let us tramp mud onto two white pieces of cloth. Then she filled two buckets with hot water and put a different detergent in each. One had phosphates in it and the other didn't. We swished them around and after a while we took the two cloths out and studied them in the sunlight. Both were spotless.

Ms. Anderson's point was that the detergent without the polluting chemical worked just as well. But when she had asked goofy Chris Wilson what he'd learned, he'd just smiled and said, "It's magic!"

Ever since then, that phrase had been a running joke. Kids who'd been in that class would say "It's magic" whenever they didn't know the answer to a question. It always got a big laugh, and the teacher always turned to someone else.

But Jennifer Peterson had no way of knowing what everyone was laughing at. She looked bewildered—and a little hurt. She must have thought everyone was laughing at *her*. If I'd been her, I would have wanted to hide under my desk or run out of the room.

Later that afternoon I was in my room working on my poster painting when the doorbell rang.

"Company for you," my mom called.

I'd decided to invite Jennifer over my house partly because I wanted to and partly because I figured it would be easier for her to bring her poem over than it would be for me to roll up a half-finished watercolor and lug it over to her house.

"Hi, Jennifer!" I looked for a car in the driveway, but there wasn't one. "How did you get here?"

"I rode my bike." She must have thought I was the world's dumbest person. Her bike was propped up against the front rail, but I'd been so busy looking for a car that I hadn't noticed it.

"All the way from Douglas Estates?" I was impressed. I'm pretty athletic myself. My speciality is running. I run nearly every day and, even if I do say so myself, I'm pretty fast. When we had done physical fitness testing at school a few weeks earlier I was the fastest runner in the whole school, boys included. Julie is kind of a jock, too. It was nice to know Jennifer had something in common with us. "That's pretty far," I said.

"It's not how far I biked that's the big deal for me," said Jennifer. "What amazes me is that I managed to get here without getting lost."

Ever since I'd gotten to know her a little better,

I'd almost forgotten that Jennifer was new in town. It must be hard finding your way around in a strange place. "How did you figure it out?" I asked.

"I looked at a map," she said matter-of-factly. "The real estate agent gave us one when we moved in."

Then I was *really* impressed. I can never make any sense at all out of maps.

Jennifer followed me into the house and began looking around. I followed her eyes as they moved from the flagstone floor of our entry hall to some of my paintings that my mother had framed and hung on the walls. Her glance came back and lingered on a wooden chest with a built-in coatrack and a funny-shaped mirror above it.

"What a cool piece of furniture," she said admiringly. "It must be very old. Is it an heirloom?"

"It belonged to my grandmother," I said. "You can hang your jacket on it if you want."

"It's so great that you use stuff like this everyday," Jennifer told me. "We have some things that belonged to my grandparents, but my mom keeps them put away so nothing happens to them. My little brother's kind of wild."

Yeah, but at least you can do homework in your living room, I said silently.

"Let's go upstairs," I suggested, rather than admit that my mother usually doesn't let me and my friends hang out in our living room.

I hurried up the staircase with Jennifer right behind me. My bedroom is the first door on the right.

"This is too much!" Jennifer cried when she saw my room.

My friends have mixed opinions on my cluttered room. It isn't large, but I like it. My favorite part is the overhead cupboards on one wall. I have to climb on a chair to use them, but they're great for storing stuff—everything from art supplies to out-of-season clothes. I painted the doors yellow and the doorknobs blue. The rest of the walls are white. In my spare time, I'm painting a border of flowers and birds around the room just above eye level. It's about two-thirds finished, and it has a lot of yellow and blue in it, plus some rose to match my rug.

I can't really use the space under the cupboards without hitting my head, so I keep big pillows on the floor there, along with a reading lamp. It's a cozy place to curl up with my homework—as long as I don't stand up too fast.

"You're so lucky! I could never get away with this in my house. And even if I did, I could never do such a great job!"

Jennifer's compliments were beginning to embarrass me.

"Maybe when you see the poster you won't think I'm so talented," I teased. It was hidden behind some blank sheets of posterboard, so I carried it to my desk and flipped on my architect's lamp.

"Pretty high-tech," Jennifer said.

"I draw here a lot and I need a good light. I know it doesn't exactly go with the rest of the decor, but . . ." I never really try to explain my bedroom to anyone. I just do whatever feels comfortable.

Jennifer leaned over my desk and studied the penciled sketch. I'd gone ahead and painted in half of the drawing.

She pointed to the big man on his hands and knees, and smiled. "This must be Bill." 'The Ransom of Red Chief' is about two kidnappers, Sam and Bill, who kidnap a little boy, Johnny Dorset, otherwise known as Red Chief.

If you've ever heard a child described as "acting like a wild Indian," you have a pretty good idea of what an uncontrollable brat Johnny is. The poor kidnappers can't wait to give him back, but they get stuck with him anyway.

I'd drawn Sam wiping his brow as he read a note that said, "Forget it. Keep him." He looked terribly confused and very woebegone. "This is Sam."

Jennifer laughed. "I love the way you drew Red Chief riding on Bill's back and hanging onto his hair. I hope my poem is funny enough to go along with this."

"Can I see it?"

Jennifer reached into her pocket and unfolded a piece of looseleaf paper. She handed it to me shyly, and looked around my room some more while I read it.

Johnny is a little creep,
A kid who no one wants to keep.
He is known as Red Chief,
And it's beyond belief,
But he's so terribly, horribly bad,
That kidnappers can't ransom him back to his dad!
If ever the punishment fit the crime,
That's surely what happened once upon *this* time
When two big rough and ready gangsters
Were taught a lesson by a pipsqueak prankster.

"I don't usually write rhyming poems," Jennifer said, "but I thought it would be funnier and more in keeping with the story if this one sounded kind of sing-song."

I thought it was great—it summed up the story, and it was funny. I especially liked the way she used the word *creep* in the very first sentence. It set the right tone.

"Jennifer, it's perfect," I said. "I really like it."

"You do?"

"Yes. I could never have written anything like this. I'm good in math and I can draw," I said, "but when it comes to writing, forget it!"

"I guess we make a good team, then."

"Ms. Lombardi is not my favorite person in the world," I giggled, "but maybe she actually knew what she was doing when she put us together. Let's figure out where to put the poem on the poster."

Of course I'd known that we were going to need

to fit a poem somewhere on the poster, but when I'd designed it, I just couldn't help filling up all the space. I twirled my hair around my finger while I looked at the poster and tried to picture the words in different positions.

"Should I put it in the middle?" I asked.

"And cover your beautiful artwork?" Jennifer was horrified.

"What if . . ." I rummaged around for a ruler. "What if we fit the first part—the part that ends with the word *dad*—over here on the left in the space next to Sam's head?" There was a little bit of sky and clouds in that part of the sketch, so the words wouldn't be covering anything important. "Then we can put the last part to the right of Sam, over Bill's head."

"I think it will look great. But won't you mind writing over your painting?"

"I knew we'd be writing on it when I made it, Jennifer. Besides, I think it makes the picture even funnier once you know what's really going on. If you'd like, I can print the words with my calligraphy pens, so the lettering will look really nice."

"I feel like I'm not doing anything," Jennifer protested.

"No, you really did a big part of this. I can draw really quickly, but it would have taken me a week to come up with a poem. And even in a week, it never would have been this good."

All I had left to do was to finish painting the poster

and then add the poem to it. I could do that anytime in the next few days. Once again, Jennifer and I had pretty much finished our work ahead of schedule.

"Do you like Bastille?" I asked, naming my favorite rock group—four people who had nothing to do with France.

"Yeah! All my friends in Minnesota do, too. Are they popular here?" Jennifer took three steps backward and sat on the edge of my bed.

"It depends on who you ask. I think they're the best, but Allie loves Vermilion and Becky is a big Jesse Barrett fan."

I popped my favorite Bastille tape into my cassette player. Then I climbed onto the bed next to Jennifer. I crossed my legs and pulled Divine, my stuffed pink flamingo, into my lap.

"Are things any better for you at school?" I asked.

Jennifer turned to face me, tucking her feet beneath her. "Do you have to ask? You were in Ms. Lombardi's class this afternoon. When Casey wasn't barking at me, everyone else was laughing."

The whole episode had slipped my mind. All of a sudden I felt terrible that I hadn't tried to catch up to Jennifer after class and explain everything to her. I told her the story about Chris and the "magic" of two different detergents each getting a cloth equally clean.

"You mean they weren't laughing at me?"

"They would have laughed even if Ms. Lombardi had said those words."

"I wish there really were such a thing as magic," Jennifer said. "I'd turn Casey Wyatt into a big fat frog. With him, it would probably be an improvement."

I *almost* felt sorry for Casey. I've heard Julie get in some good comebacks when Casey bothers her, but it sounded like Jennifer could top them anytime. Still, Casey is such a jerk, he couldn't possibly get worse than he deserved.

"No one likes Casey Wyatt," I said. "At least, none of the girls do."

"You mean he's like that with everyone?" She sounded surprised.

"Worse," I said. "You know, he's best friends with Mark Harris—"

"Is he Julie Berger's boyfriend?" Jennifer interrupted.

"I don't know," I giggled. "Julie has a big crush on him and he seems to like her, but I don't think anything's official. Anyway, Casey used to call Julie all kinds of rotten names, like Tinsel Teeth and Brace Face. Especially when Mark was around, because he knew Mark liked Julie."

"Oh, how horrible!" Jennifer covered her face with her hands.

"Casey's a total dweeb," I said. "Everyone in that class has heard worse from him than you did today." That reminded me. "Hey, Jennifer? What was that word you said in class today—oof dah or something like that? Were you cursing?"

"No!" Now it was Jennifer's turn to laugh. "I said *uff da*. It doesn't really mean anything. It's just a word that people in Minnesota use. It means different things depending upon how you use it, but mostly it means something like 'oops.' "

"Uff da," I repeated. "Maybe I'll start using it. We might start a new trend in Canfield," I mused.

"Well, that would be a nice change," Jennifer said.

"Speaking of changes," I said, "I know we talked about me showing you some different ways to put outfits together. . . ." I gulped and added, "And I was wondering if maybe you'd like me to give you a makeover."

"I'd love it!" Jennifer said. "You want to do it now?"

I was so relieved she wasn't insulted! "It's probably better if we do it at your house," I said, "because then I can look at your wardrobe and try different combinations. It won't be any good if I come up with a new look for you that doesn't match your personal style."

"It doesn't really matter—I don't have any personal style," she said. "How did you get to be so good at this stuff?"

"I don't know. Maybe I inherited it from my mom. She owns Cinderella—"

"The shop on Main Street?" Jennifer asked before I could add any details. "I love the windows."

I flushed with pleasure. Sometimes I help my mom come up with ideas for new window displays, but I felt too self-conscious to tell Jennifer that. I'm proud of my mom's store and the really interesting clothes she sells. Especially the ones she designs herself.

"My mom and I have been there. It's my favorite store in town!" Jennifer said. "What does your dad do?"

"He's a lawyer. Have you heard of Torres and Kaplan?"

"No," she giggled. "I haven't needed a lawyer yet. Seriously, though, my dad might know him. He works for Selby International. He's vice president of product development."

Selby International was an enormous company that had offices all over the country. I guessed her father had been transferred from a branch in Minnesota to the company headquarters in Vermont.

"Does your mom give you lots of clothes ideas?" Jennifer asked.

"Not really," I said. "In fact, sometimes she just looks at some of the stuff I've come up with and shakes her head."

"Well, I'll let you know if I don't like anything you do in my makeover," Jennifer laughed.

That reminded me of something I needed to warn Jennifer about. "Um, Jennifer," I began, "I should tell you that the last time I did a really big makeover, it was on Julie Berger."

Jennifer looked at me expectantly. "What did Julie look like *before* the makeover?"

"Well, her hair was a lot longer," I said slowly.

Jennifer grabbed her own long hair as if she thought I might whip out a pair of scissors and give her a mohawk.

"Don't worry," I said. "I won't cut your hair! But I may try to come up with some different hairstyles."

"Sounds fine," Jennifer said. "Can we do it tomorrow?"

The next day was our special shopping trip for Julie's birthday. No way would Becky and Allie expect Jennifer to come along. "I can't do it tomorrow," I said. Jennifer looked a little disappointed, so I quickly added, "How about Saturday?"

"You're on," Jennifer said. "That's even better, really, because we'll have a lot more time if we need it. After all, I want you to make me look like Paula Abdul, and it might take a while." I checked to make sure Jennifer was kidding but she looked very serious. I was beginning to worry that she really meant it when she cracked up. "Sorry, just teasing," she said.

"She seems like a nice girl," my mother said on our way home from Douglas Estates. My mom had invited Jennifer to stay for dinner that evening, so after we'd finished we loaded her bicycle into the trunk of our car and dropped her off.

"I like her a lot," I said, "but . . ." I wanted to ask my mom's advice about what to do about Jennifer and the other kids at school, but I felt weird about it.

"Is something bothering you about Jennifer?" she asked.

"I like Jennifer. I mean, I haven't known her that long, but she's really nice. The trouble is, she got off on the wrong foot at school, and most of the other kids hate her."

"Hate her?" she asked.

"Well, on her first day in school she said she hated it here." Before my mom could say anything else, I rushed on, "She just had had a rotten morning and that creepy Casey Wyatt had been mean to her and I guess it just kind of burst out. But after that, no one wanted to be friends with her. She's sort of an outcast, and kids make fun of her sometimes. At lunch she never has anyone to sit with, so she sits all by herself."

"Why don't you invite her to sit with you?" my mother asked reasonably.

It was very hard to admit the truth about my friends. "Allie and Julie and Becky don't like her either. I know I should stand up for Jennifer when they make jokes about her, but it's hard."

My mom stopped at a red light and looked at me. "I imagine it's very hard."

"Am I wrong? When I feel like I should do something to help Jennifer but I don't do it, am I a bad person?" I couldn't look my mother in the eye.

My mom squeezed my hand. "No, you're not bad. It's a very awkward situation."

"What am I supposed to do?" I really hoped she would have some advice. I couldn't figure out any solution myself, and I could hardly ask my friends for ideas.

"You can't make the kids at school like Jennifer," she said. "But you could try to say something to your friends that would make them more sensitive to her feelings."

"I don't know. . . ." I couldn't see myself giving my friends lessons in how to be nice to someone.

"The most important thing for you to do right now is to be a friend to Jennifer. You could do a lot to help her adjust to Canfield."

She was right. If Jennifer felt more comfortable, she might be able to make more friends. I hoped her birthday party would help some girls get to know her better. It would be a beginning, anyway.

When we got in the house, my mom gave me a big hug. "I'm very proud of you, Rosie," she said. "I know that whatever you do will be the right thing."

Five

"On your mark, get set—shop!" Becky cried. We were cruising through the Pine Tree Mall, and we'd just gotten to The Wishbone.

The Wishbone is our favorite store. It has tons of really neat stuff, like little fake potted plants that dance to music and gigantic inflatable neon-pink flamingos. Our parents hate it, but we always get each other the best presents there.

Allie tugged on my sleeve, a worried look on her face. "I keep thinking Julie's going to walk out of one of the stores," she fretted.

"She's not," I told her. "I am absolutely sure she's home doing her biology assignment. Mrs. Berger promised me that whatever she did, she would not take Julie shopping tonight."

Allie shook her head. "But Julie loves to surprise people. And you know she's always turning up where you least expect her."

"Tell me about it. Last night, while I was working on her card, she decided to stop over and surprise me. My mom let her in but didn't tell me she was here. The next thing I knew, she was standing in the doorway."

"Oh no!" Becky exclaimed. "Did she see the card?"

"I said it was an art project and I stuffed it into my notebook."

"What did she want? Do you think she—" Allie paused for dramatic effect—"*suspects* anything about the party?"

"No," I said. "She just wanted to catch up on things because she's been so busy lately. I told her we'd go over everything at the Party Line meeting Sunday, so we just hung out for a while."

We were wandering through the aisles, looking at all the cool things we could get Julie, when Becky suddenly cried, "Eureka!"

"What? What?" Allie and I were trying to see what Becky was clutching in her hand.

"It's perfect, isn't it?" Becky held out a gold-colored keychain. At one end was a regular keyring, and at the other was a tiny model of a shocking pink Corvette convertible. If ever a car had Julie's name on it, that one did.

"Julie has a keychain," Allie said, practical as ever. "How could you forget it, Becky?" Julie's keychain was a five-inch-long hollow plastic shark filled with liquid glitter.

"Yes, but she doesn't have one for her *car* keys," Becky said triumphantly.

"Because she doesn't have a car!" Allie retorted.

I got it, though. It was a really clever gift when

you thought about it. "Allie, remember our party theme?" I asked.

"Oh, right," Allie said, blushing faintly. "We're celebrating her entry into adulthood, so we give her a keychain for when she's old enough to drive."

"I can't wait until I can drive," Becky said with a sigh.

"Let me know when that day comes so I can stay home," I teased. Everyone knew Becky had klutz attacks without any warning.

"Very funny. I'll be a great driver."

Allie said seriously, "She's probably right. Once Becky makes her mind up to do something, that's it." Allie was right. Becky has so many ideas that I sometimes wonder how they all fit inside her head. And when she decides to go for something, everyone might as well just get out of her way. She's famous for barreling ahead on things that most people would spend weeks thinking about. But no matter how impulsive she seems, she always does everything perfectly once she makes up her mind.

"Becky, I take it back," I said.

She grinned. "Just for that, I promise to give you rides when I get my license."

"Thanks," I said.

We hadn't found anything else that was really right, and so we were waiting at the cash register when I saw it: a mauve-colored address book with a bird of paradise design all over it. It was small enough to tuck in a pocket, and it looked very feminine.

I was fingering the little book when I caught Allie's eye.

"A book for Julie to put all her boyfriends' phone numbers in?" Allie asked, grinning.

Becky snorted. She still didn't think much of boys, but I wondered about Allie. It seemed to me as if she was really starting to get interested in them herself, and I made a mental note to keep an eye on her. I guess Julie wasn't the only one growing up.

We bought the book and the keychain and strolled back into the mall.

We decided to go to Winter's department store next. Since the entrance was right near the lingerie section, we went there first. There were racks and racks of lacy underwear and nightgowns. The greatest thing we saw was a black lace camisole and matching bikini set. It was too expensive for us to give it to Julie, however, and her mother would have gone into a coma anyway if she'd seen it.

"Still, it would've been a fabulous gift," I said as we lingered near the display. Becky lifted up the camisole and crossed her eyes at me through the lace.

"Peek-a-boo," she trilled in a falsetto voice. I couldn't help cracking up, and neither could Allie. A salesperson looked at us, and we quickly moved to the other end of the department.

We walked around looking at silk kimonos, fluffy

robes, and little lacy jackets trimmed with fur. Then Allie pulled a hanger out of a rack of nightgowns.

I'd never seen a more beautiful nightgown. It was lavender, made of a silky material that felt as soft as a teddy bear. It came to the floor and had two thin straps made of lavender lace.

I couldn't help touching it. I held it up against my chest and watched the material swirl around my legs.

"How much is it?" I breathed.

Allie beamed. "It's only twenty-two dollars," she said. "We can do it."

We'd each decided to chip in ten dollars toward Julie's presents. Normally we didn't spend that much on each other, but Julie's bat mitzvah was a super-special occasion. Plus with the money we earned from our Party Line jobs, we could afford to spend that much.

The keychain cost two-fifty and the little address book was three-fifty. Even with tax, we still had more than twenty-three dollars left.

I think the salesperson was shocked that we actually bought something. "It's a present," I told her. "Could you put it in a gift box?" The satiny gift box came with its own sparkly ivory bow, so we didn't even have to spend money for gift wrap.

We'd done all our official shopping, so we spent the next hour doing what we usually do—we just walked around and looked at different stuff and tried to imagine what sorts of outfits we could come up

with if we could ever afford some of the really terrific clothes we saw.

Allie stopped near a fringed suede vest. I couldn't
imagine Allie ever wearing something like that, and
I was surprised she was even interested in it. Then
I remembered that Vermilion wore one just like it
in her new video. Allie caught me looking at her and
sighed.

"Someday," she said, pointing to the price tag. The
vest cost a hundred and forty-five dollars!

Becky, meanwhile, was busy trying to wrap a
feather boa around her neck. It was made from wispy
little feathers and was dyed an outrageous shade of
purple. As she tossed one end over her shoulder it
floated down slowly, as if it were as light as air.

"Can you believe they still make these things?"
Becky asked. "I thought women stopped wearing
these years ago."

"Not at all," said a salesperson who'd suddenly
come up behind Becky. "They're very glamorous,
and make a lovely accent for evening wear."

Becky said, "Oh, really?" and, when the sales-
woman wasn't looking, rolled her eyes at me. She
put the boa back on the counter and we took off.

As we approached the cosmetics counter, Becky
and Allie automatically slowed their pace. They
knew it was nearly impossible for me to pass without stopping.

That's when I saw the special kit on display. It

had ten different eyeshadows, four blushes, and four little pots of lip gloss in it.

"This is new!" I said. I could do a lot with a kit like that. "Do we have time for a makeover?" I asked. That is my favorite thing to do when we all go shopping together. My friends are used to it, and never seem to mind being guinea pigs for my latest makeup ideas. Most of the time they turn out pretty well, anyway.

Allie looked longingly at the colorful case. Becky looked at her watch. I think she was about to say we didn't have time when she saw Allie's face. "If you're quick, Rosie," she told me.

So I gave Allie a mini-transformation with a little pink blush, a tiny bit of pale blue eyeshadow that almost matched her eyes, and rose-colored lip gloss. I think it was my best look yet for Allie.

She seemed really happy with it, too. *If only I could get her to wear makeup like that when Dylan Matthews is around*, I thought, *he'd realize how pretty Allie is*. Allie looked kind of dreamy as we left the counter, and I wondered if she was thinking the same thing.

Becky had been sniffing the perfume testers while I worked on Allie. She held one up and spritzed it in the air near us.

"Mmm. That smells heavenly," I murmured.

Allie took the bottle and sprayed some on her wrist. Then she peered at the label. "Island Gardens. I don't know what islands have to do with it, but it does smell good."

"It's too bad we spent all our money," Becky said. "I was thinking this would be perfect for—"

"Julie!" we all said at once.

"Oh, it *is* too bad," said Allie. "You're right. It's perfect."

The salesperson behind the perfume counter smiled at us. "Island Gardens is sixty dollars an ounce," she said.

We all gasped. "It's okay, we never could have afforded it anyway," Becky told her.

"I do have a sample I could give you," the salesperson went on. "I couldn't help overhearing you say that this would be perfect for your friend."

We couldn't believe it! Usually the salespeople were nice to us, but it was obvious they thought we were just kids and weren't going to buy anything big. This woman was really different.

She handed us an elegant little gold envelope. Inside was a tiny golden flask with a few drops of Island Gardens inside it.

"Thanks!" we said.

"It's for a really special occasion and our friend will love it," I added.

We were all talking excitedly as we left the store about how nice that salesperson had been and how the perfume sample would make a great gift for Julie. I guess none of us were looking where we were going, because suddenly Allie collided with someone—someone who turned out to be Dylan Matthews!

"Excuse me," he said, although it was our fault. *At least he has nice manners,* I thought.

"Oh, excuse me," Allie gasped. "I'm so sorry." Allie was gazing at him as if they were the only two people in the world. And I noticed he wasn't looking at anyone else, either.

"Uh, well, I guess I'll see you in school," he said.

"Yeah. See you in school," Allie said.

I was dying to ask Allie a million questions, but something in Becky's face told me to shut up. Allie looked positively blissful. I wondered if my makeover had caused Dylan to pay a little more attention to Allie. Whatever it was, he sure looked interested.

If only I could manage to do the same for Jennifer the next day.

Six

"Ready?" I asked. Jennifer nodded.

We were in Jennifer's room. The Petersons' living room was great, but it wasn't exactly the place to give someone a makeover.

Jennifer's room was ideal, though. It was a corner room, and each outside wall had two tall windows set in narrow alcoves that ran from floor to ceiling. The wallpaper looked like an English garden, covered with roses in every color from pale pink to burgundy. The four-poster bed had a white eyelet canopy and a matching bedspread. I thought I'd never seen anything so romantic.

I lined up my makeover materials on her little white and gold vanity table. Jennifer had washed her face and tied back her hair, and was sitting in the delicate-looking chair that matched the table.

I stood in front of the chair and studied her.

"You look like an artist surveying her blank canvas," Jennifer told me.

"I'm just trying to figure out the right way to highlight your best features," I said. "Your eyes are a wonderful shade of blue, so I want to be careful not to do anything that will distract from them."

I thought Jennifer's pale skin could use a little more color, so I tried a bronze-colored blush. It was a big mistake. She looked like an orange-skinned alien.

Jennifer didn't say anything, but I caught her eye in the mirror. We both started laughing.

"Okay, so this isn't the blush for you," I said as I patted some cold cream on her face and tissued off the grisly-looking color. "Sometimes you have to try a few different shades to see what looks best."

"What was your biggest makeover disaster?" Jennifer asked.

"You mean besides Julie's hair?"

"That's right, I'd forgotten about Julie's hair. You said it used to be longer. What happened?"

I told her the whole awful story, how I'd tried to give Julie a new look and kept clipping and clipping to even the sides until it was obvious it was hopeless. Even after a professional haircutter had evened it up, Julie was still miserable. She was so upset I thought she'd never speak to me again.

"But Julie's hair looks adorable," Jennifer protested.

"Yes, and now Julie thinks so, too," I said. "But it was pretty touchy for a few days. I thought I'd lost my best friend."

Jennifer gave me a sympathetic look. I guessed that she'd left *her* best friend in Minnesota.

"Do you still talk with your friends from home?" I asked.

"It's really expensive to call, so we only do it once in a while," Jennifer said. "Mostly we write to each other. But it isn't the same."

I felt bad for her, but I didn't know what to say.

Jennifer picked up one of my blush compacts and looked at it. "This is a pretty shade of pink," she said.

Relieved to have something to do, I leaned over and took it from her hands. "Let's see how this looks," I said.

It was exactly the perfect color for Jennifer. It made her look like one of those beautiful porcelain dolls, with complexions the color of rosebuds and cream.

"See?" I said. "You have good color sense. You just need to have more confidence in it."

Jennifer looked pleased.

I found a slightly darker pink gloss for her lips. So far, so good.

I tried some baby-blue eyeshadow on her upper eyelid, and stood back to survey her critically. I shook my head. Very carefully, I brushed a cotton swab dipped in baby oil along Jennifer's eyelids to remove it.

"What was wrong with that color?" Jennifer asked. "I thought it looked okay."

"That's what was wrong with it," I told her. "It looked only okay. The blue of the shadow was com-

peting with the blue of your eyes, instead of comple-
menting it."

"Leave it to an artist to see that," Jennifer
laughed.

Finally I selected a deep violet eyeshadow and
brushed it very lightly above Jennifer's eyes. I even
dabbed at it with a cotton ball to remove any excess.
I wanted to give her eyes just a hint of color.

I gently tipped her eyelashes with black mascara,
just to darken the very ends, which are usually
lighter than the rest of the lash. Her lashes didn't
look gunky at all; they just looked long and silky,
the way they should look. I really don't like to see
people wearing gobs of makeup. Some people cake
their eyelashes with gluey-looking mascara, and I
think it looks gross. As much as I love to fool around
with cosmetics, I guess I'm really a less-is-more person. I think a person should use just enough makeup to make her features stand out, and not a bit
more than that.

I could tell Jennifer was impressed so far. So was
I, actually. I knew she was pretty and that she could
look a lot better than she usually did. But I had to
admit that she was my best makeover to date. She
looked amazingly beautiful once I was done with the
makeup.

I had a feeling that at least part of Jennifer's new
look was more than skin-deep, though. Part of it was
that Jennifer was starting to feel more comfortable
with me, and so she smiled and laughed a lot more.

I know it sounds corny, but I think it really is true that the better you feel, the better you look.

"You're so good at this, Rosie. You should move to Hollywood and do makeup for movie stars someday."

"Hollywood . . . hmm." I'd always thought that when I turned sixteen I'd try to get a job working at Winter's cosmetic counter, but Jennifer's idea was a lot more interesting.

"Hey, Rosie?" Jennifer looked serious all of a sudden. "My mom told me The Party Line is going to do my birthday party."

I don't know why I was startled. After all, Mrs. Peterson hadn't said it was supposed to be a surprise party.

Jennifer was quick to explain, though. "Usually my mom asks me what I want to do on my birthday—whether I want a party or to do something special. It's sort of a Peterson family tradition. So when she didn't say anything, I asked her. And she told me she'd hired you guys."

"Do you mind?" I asked.

"I think it's great!" Jennifer said. "But I want to know one thing: you're going to actually be there, right? I mean, you'll be there as guests even though you're also giving the party, won't you?"

"Well," I said, "we have to be there to run the games and bring out the cake and stuff, but usually we're not guests since the parties are almost always for small kids. The only party we ever did for someone our age was for a boy, so there wasn't really any question of our being there as guests—although we did end up playing softball with the guys."

"Who was the party for?" Jennifer asked curiously.

I wrinkled my nose. "Casey Wyatt."

"Casey Wyatt! I thought you couldn't stand him!" Jennifer cried.

"I can't!" I said.

"Then why'd you do a party for him?" Jennifer asked. She looked puzzled.

"We had to," I explained. "Julie, of all people, was the one who got us into it. She thought it was for Casey's little brother ... until we told her Casey didn't have a little brother. Then it was too late to back out."

"Ooh, that must have been awful," Jennifer said.

"It was even worse when Casey found out," I told her. "He started a boys-against-girls feud in school and everything. The party turned out pretty good, though."

"So will you guys be guests at my party, or what?" Jennifer asked.

"You bet. Your mom told us that even though we were actually giving the party, she expected us to be part of it as well."

"Good. That's what I told her to tell you." Jennifer grinned.

"Ready for the hair portion of your makeover?"

Jennifer pulled her hair out of the ponytail. There

were lots of things she could do with her long hair, but she almost always just wore it tied back. Boring.

I parted it down the center and then used a comb to draw a line down to each ear, sectioning off the hair on each side of her face. I twisted those sections and pulled them to the back of her head, where I fastened them with a pretty little barrette Jennifer had in one of her drawers.

It looked cute. Jennifer's hair was out of her eyes, but it still hung long and smooth on either side of her face.

"I like it," Jennifer said. "It's easy enough for me to do before school in the morning, but it's not as . . ."

"Boring?" I supplied, realizing too late what I was saying.

Jennifer laughed. "It's okay, Rosie. You're right, it *is* boring just to pull my hair back in a ponytail. But it's also easy, and it does keep my hair out of my face."

"Do you know how to make a French braid?" I asked her.

"No, but I've always wanted to," she said.

I showed her how to do it, combing her hair into sections and then weaving it into a long, full braid.

"Do you have any hair ribbons?"

Jennifer opened another drawer and pointed. It was full of all sorts of ribbons and headbands and scrunchy hair elastics. I'd never seen so many in one place except at a hairdresser's—and I'd never seen Jennifer wear any of the hair ornaments I found there. I chose a watered blue silk ribbon and tied the braid just below the back of her neck.

"This is great!" she declared. "The only thing is, I'm not sure I could do this myself every morning. Maybe I'll just save it for special occasions."

I went to undo the braid.

"You're not going to take it out!" Jennifer cried.

"I thought I'd try one more hairstyle on you," I said. "I can always rebraid your hair when we're done, if you'd like."

"Okay."

The next style I tried was parting Jennifer's hair on the side and pulling part of it up in a clip. It looked pretty good, too.

"It's always a good idea to know how to do more than one hairstyle," I told her. "Then you can change back and forth for different looks. You're lucky to have such nice long hair."

Finally I rebraided her hair. But that time I did a French braid on the side, so it fell over one shoulder. I think that was my favorite style.

Jennifer liked it best, too. "The great thing about a side braid is that it's a lot easier to do yourself. This way, I'll be able to see what I'm doing and I won't have to reach all the way behind my head.

"What do you think of bangs?" she went on. "I've been thinking about them, but I just don't know."

"If it involves cutting hair, don't even ask me about it!" I said, laughing. "No, really. I think bangs might look good, but you wouldn't be able to do as many different things with your hair."

"I'll keep thinking about it." Jennifer got up and walked over to a set of big double doors on one wall. She opened them all the way to reveal an enormous walk-in closet. One side had dresses and jackets, and the other side had a row of blouses hanging high above wide shelves that held a a riot of colorful sweaters and sweat clothes.

"Wow," I said. I was amazed. Jennifer had great stuff hiding in her closet.

I picked up a light blue sweater with snowflakes knitted all over it. No two were alike, either. "Why haven't you ever worn this?"

"It's too big."

"Big sweaters look great. Try it on," I told her.

It looked great on her. The sleeves fell just past her wrists and the bottom of the sweater reached almost to her knees.

"You could even wear it as a dress with tights," I marveled. "You might want to roll up the sleeves a little, but you don't even need to."

"It does look good," Jennifer agreed.

I found a pair of slim white leggings rolled up on one of the shelves. When I handed them to Jennifer, she admitted, "I don't like the way they make my stomach look. They're all baggy and saggy in front."

"So hide that part," I suggested.

Once she'd put them on, we looked in the big full-length mirror on the back of her bedroom door.

"Hey, nice!"

The sweater covered the part of the pants that looked funny. All you could see were the skinny white leggings topped by a fabulous big sweater. As we looked into the mirror, I pushed the sleeves up to her elbows. I thought it looked a lot better that way.

"What do you think?" I asked.

"I never thought of putting these two things together. What else can we try?"

We spent the next hour mixing and matching shirts and sweaters with pants and skirts. I knew I had never seen half of her clothes. I fell in love with a small navy corduroy vest. It had delicate embroidery along its edges, and the back was made from a silky fabric printed with birds and flowers.

I tried it on. "Where did you get this?"

Jennifer got a faraway look in her eyes. "My best friend back in Rock Valley made it for me. Four of us had them."

"Matching?" Talk about having close friends! Not even Julie, Allie, Becky, and I dress alike.

"Just cut from the same pattern. Beth's was checked in the front and had plaid black silk in back. Marie's was made of paisley printed material with a different paisley pattern for the back. And Samantha's was shocking pink corduroy. You'd have to know Sam to know how perfect *that* was for her."

It sounded so fun. I could almost see them shopping together to choose their material. Both the look in her eyes and the sad ring to her words made me realize just how much Jennifer had left behind her in Minnesota. She hadn't always eaten lunch alone or said the wrong things in class.

Rather than make her more sad by asking questions about Samantha and the others, I asked, "Why haven't you worn any of these clothes to school?"

Jennifer turned away from the mirror. "I grew over the summer and since my mom knew we'd be moving, we didn't buy many new clothes for fall. She thought the girls might dress differently here and that it would make more sense to do our shopping in Canfield."

I surveyed the clothes spread across her bed. Some did look like things I'd seen at Winter's and other stores in the mall.

Jennifer must have read my mind. "Yeah, a lot of these clothes are new, but it's more comfortable to wear my old stuff—at least the things that still fit."

"Even if it . . ." I couldn't finish my question. Was I supposed to tell her we all thought her clothes looked funny?

Jennifer blushed. "I just haven't wanted to wear the new clothes. I guess I've been a little afraid."

"Afraid?" I couldn't imagine being scared to try something new. I was always experimenting with styles.

"I'm not the biggest chicken in the world, if that's what you're thinking," Jennifer informed me. "But I'm not brave enough to try new things when all the kids laugh at me."

I understood immediately. She didn't feel safe at Canfield. Even if I put together a truly horrible outfit, my friends wouldn't tease me. They probably wouldn't let anyone else insult me either. But Jennifer couldn't count on anyone to support her. Although her new clothes didn't look funny to me, they were probably new styles for her, and she was reluctant to try them out in such a hostile environment.

"I wonder which Jennifer Peterson I'll see at school Monday," I said lightly.

"You'll just have to wait and see," Jennifer answered with a smile.

Seven

"Okay, let's get to work!" Becky pushed the sleeves of her brother's Canfield High sweatshirt up to her elbows.

"Aye, aye, Madame President," Julie saluted.

Our Sunday afternoon Party Line meetings often start this way. President Becky enjoys her work. None of us mind it when she takes control, because she's the best one for the job. (And if she gets *too* bossy, well, *ve haf vays* of making her stop!)

Becky does have the best ideas, though. And she doesn't let us fool around—at least not too much—until our work is finished.

Becky grinned. "The topic today is the Jennifer Peterson party scheduled for . . ." She hesitated and frowned. "A week from this Saturday."

My friends groaned. Julie had a suggestion. "Maybe we should tell Mrs. Peterson we're all very sick and can't do the job."

"But we've never let anyone down before." Allie didn't seem to realize Julie was kidding.

"I don't think that's funny, Julie," I said.

"What's with you?" Julie asked, surprised.

"I'm just tired of hearing everyone complain about this party. When you accepted the Casey Wyatt job, we all pitched in and the party turned out okay. I accepted the Jennifer Peterson job. And I wish you'd just get used to the idea and help make it work."

Julie looked even more surprised. I usually don't speak up like that—not to anyone, and especially not to Julie. But Julie understood how I felt.

"You're right, Rosie," she said, immediately contrite. "I'm sorry I've been acting like such a jerk about it."

"Hear, hear," Becky said, tossing an unopened bag of cheddar cheese popcorn at Julie. Leave it to Becky to get us all over a tough moment. Nothing distracts Julie better than food, either.

"This meeting is called to order," Becky went on. "The suspense has been killing me. We are here to hear Rosie Torres's ideas for a 'Welcome to Canfield' party."

"And to contribute any ideas if you have them," I added.

"Well?" Allie asked.

I crossed my legs on the small and somewhat threadbare Oriental carpet beneath me. We hold our meetings in Becky's attic. Together we had cleared a spot in the center of the cluttered top floor of the house and covered the creaky floorboards with old rugs and oversized pillows. It's a very comfortable and cozy place to hang out.

"Are you going to share your ideas? Or are they personal?" Julie teased.

I cleared my throat. "We all know Jennifer is new to Canfield. Since we've been working together on the English project, I've learned how much she misses her old school and her friends back home. The move has been especially hard for her because she hasn't gotten to know many people—"

"No surprise," Julie interrupted. "We all know she hasn't made any friends. That's half our problem."

"Whose fault is it she hasn't made friends?" Becky asked. "She's such a snob. I couldn't believe she just ignored me and Allie the other day."

"When?" Julie asked, very interested.

"We were walking home from school one day," Becky said quickly. "The day your mom picked you up right after school." It was a white lie, but it probably wasn't the first one we'd have to tell in order to keep the surprise party a secret.

"Well, she felt weird because you and Allie kept staring at her," I said. "And it kind of intimidated her, so she was afraid to say hello."

"How do you know?" Becky demanded.

"She told me," I said simply.

"She did?" Allie was astonished.

"She felt bad about it," I told her.

"I guess we were staring at that outrageous sweater," Becky admitted.

"Jennifer *could* make friends, and our party can

help," I rushed on. "That's why I think a 'Welcome to Canfield' party is a good idea. What if everyone wears their Canfield Middle School sweatshirts? You know, the ones we all got last year for participating in the school's fiftieth-anniversary celebration."

Becky smiled. "I like it. It's a cheap way to set the mood."

"Have you considered what the party will cost?" Allie asked.

"Of course. I'm the treasurer!" I pulled out my sheet of figures. "I told Mrs. Peterson we'd charge about a hundred and fifty dollars for a teenage party. That's a little more than the Casey Wyatt party, but Mrs. Peterson wants us to make this one really special."

"That's a lot of money, even after you take out our fifty percent profit," Allie said, skimming her finger down one of her party organization sheets.

We have a system for figuring out party costs. First, we add up how much it will cost to buy the party supplies—everything from invitations and decorations to snacks and cake. Then we take half that cost and add it to our bill. That way we're sure to make a profit.

We put ten percent of our profit in our treasury. We divide the other forty percent among us, which works out very neatly since there are four of us.

"It is a lot of money, but it will cost a lot of money to put together a really good party. Not only that, but Mrs. Peterson said she's willing to spend even more if we need it," I said.

"Whew," Allie sighed. Once Allie forgot to add in our profit and we almost ended up losing money on a party. The woman who hired us that time figured out that we'd undercharged her and volunteered to make up the difference. It was a good thing, too, because we never would have gone back on our word and asked her for more money. So it was nice to know that we were covered in case we overspent on Jennifer's party.

"Plus," I went on, "she's offered us extra money to buy a special gift for each guest."

"Really?" Allie squealed. "What a great idea!"

"Let's see if we can come up with a good party favor," said Becky. "What's a cool thing we can get that won't cost too much money?"

"Does it matter what we spend?" Julie asked.

"I don't think Mrs. Peterson will really care too much as long as it's under ten dollars," I said.

"Ten dollars!" Allie yelled.

"But I think we should try to keep it around three dollars, don't you? We should try to keep expenses down. This way, if we need to ask for more money for the actual party stuff, it won't seem like we're being really extravagant." I didn't want Mrs. Peterson to think we were taking advantage of her generosity.

"You're right," Becky said. "I'd rather spend more on the party itself than have an expensive favor."

"What about keychains?" Julie asked.

Becky, Allie, and I looked at each other. Could Julie possibly have had any idea about our secret shopping trip?

"Oh, no," gasped Allie.

"You think it's a bad idea?" Julie asked, completely oblivious to what was going on.

"Well, I mean," Becky said glibly, "they probably all have keychains anyway. Let's try to come up with something else."

"What about nail polish?" I asked. "We could give everyone a little bottle of nail polish, each one a different color. Then people can trade if they don't like the color they got."

"Oh, Rosie! Only you would think that's a great gift!" Becky snorted.

"That's not true," Allie said. "I wouldn't mind nail polish."

"Well, I would!" said Becky emphatically. "I *never* wear it, and I'm not about to start."

"Me, either," said Julie. "I like it on other people, but I just don't have the patience to do it myself."

"Okay, okay," I said. "Forget the nail polish."

"What about friendship bracelets?" asked Julie. "No one ever has enough of those."

"That's a great idea!" Becky said enthusiastically.

"But they only cost around two dollars each," Allie said. "Do you think that's kind of cheap for a party favor?"

"Well, it's better than no party favor at all!" Becky said.

"Allie may be right," I said. "Maybe two dollars is a little too inexpensive, but I don't think we should spend more than three dollars altogether. What should we do?"

"I know," said Julie. "Let's give them friendship bracelets and sunglass holders. Sunglass holders only cost about a dollar or a dollar-fifty. And they're really cool, too."

"And The Wishbone has them in all sorts of wild fluorescent colors!" Becky finished happily.

"They do?" Julie asked. "I haven't seen them there."

"That's right," Allie said. "I saw them by the counter the other day—" She broke off suddenly and began to blush furiously.

My heart sank. There was almost no chance Julie would let that remark go by. I knew when she had come over so unexpectedly a few days earlier that she was beginning to feel a little left out of things. With all the things she had to do to get ready for her bat mitzvah, she hadn't been able to spend much time with us. It would have been terrible if she had thought we were doing fun stuff without her.

"You guys went to the mall without me?" Julie demanded. "Some friends you are!"

"We d-d-didn't all go," Allie said quickly. "My mom had to g-g-get something for Mouse, and I went with her. I j-j-just happened to notice them, that's all. And I told Becky about them." Allie's stammer made it obvious that she was rattled over her slip.

"Berger, will you quit being paranoid?" Becky said. "You think we've been planning secret shopping trips without you? What do you think we are, a bunch of traitors?"

Julie giggled. "I'm sorry," she said. "It's just that I feel so out of touch lately."

"The price you pay for growing up," Becky teased wickedly.

Julie made a rude noise. "Better than staying a child," she said pointedly. Then she and Becky slammed pillows at each other at the same time, and fell over laughing hysterically.

Allie looked genuinely bewildered. "Are they fighting, or what?" she asked me.

"They're proving that neither of them is as grown-up as she thinks she is," I said with a grin. Julie and Becky leaped up and simultaneously sent their pillows winging my way.

"Okay, truce!" I cried.

Becky sat up and attempted to smooth her hair. "Okay, let's get back to business," she said briskly. Only Becky could be rolling around on the floor one minute, then playing Madame President the next. "Have we got any idea who we'll invite?" she asked.

"We'd better figure that out soon," said Allie. "We really should hand out invitations in school sometime this week. Otherwise we'll be cutting it much too close."

"She's right," I admitted.

I was surprised when Julie suddenly got very businesslike. She'd been scribbling on her pad, and she tore the sheet off and handed it to me.

"Here," she said. "I think all these people will come. Especially if we explain that it's a 'Welcome to Canfield' party when we hand them their invitations."

Julie had made a list of all the girls in our class.

"Thanks." I smiled at her. She was trying to make up for giving me a hard time, and I appreciated it.

"You know, Jennifer doesn't exactly have a great reputation in class," Becky pointed out. "I think a lot of people still hold those anti-Canfield remarks against her."

"I guess we'll just have to explain as best as we can and hope for the best," I said lamely.

"As far as Jennifer's concerned, it's a 'Welcome to Canfield' party." Becky said. "But as far as everyone else is concerned, it'll be a 'Give Jennifer a Second Chance' party."

"We're guests *and* givers at this one, right?" Allie asked me.

"Yes, Mrs. Peterson wants it that way—and so does Jennifer," I explained.

"Jennifer wants us as guests?"

"That's what she told me," I said.

"Can we all go shopping after school tomorrow for party supplies?" Becky asked.

A chorus of yeses confirmed the shopping trip.

We spent about five more minutes coming up with a list of all the things we'd need to buy, including a Canfield Middle School sweatshirt for Jennifer, and the rest of the time listening to everything Julie had been up to.

"When is your bat mitzvah again?" Becky asked, as if we didn't all have it marked in big red letters on our calendars. When Julie wasn't looking, Becky gave me and Allie a big wink.

"It's in three weeks," Julie said. "Less than that, actually. It's a week after Jennifer's party. Didn't you get your invitations yet?"

"Oh, that's right," Becky said, as if she'd just made the connection.

"Are you guys all losing your minds or something?" Julie wanted to know.

"We've been pretty busy lately," I said.

"Doing what?" Julie asked.

"Oh, you know, school and things," Allie said carelessly.

Julie started talking about other things then, and we breathed a collective sigh of relief. Our secret was still safe!

Eight

"What happened to *her*?"

Heads turned when Jennifer walked into English class Monday morning. Even I took a second look.

She was wearing the first outfit we'd put together during our makeover session on Saturday, the blue snowflake sweater with the white leggings. Her hair was in a French braid on the side with white and blue ribbons woven in. The combination of clothes, cosmetics, and accessories really made her look like a new person.

It wasn't just a change on the outside. She seemed happier and livelier and brighter. Her eyes were sparkling and she was actually smiling!

There were a few things about the new Jennifer that I hadn't seen at her house. Her white satin ballet shoes each had a tiny blue snowflake embroidered on the toe. They hadn't been in her closet; she and her mom must have shopped after I went home. I hadn't suggested the ribbons or the terrific hoop earrings, either.

Some people were staring at her as she walked to

her desk and sat down, as if they were trying to figure out what was so new and different about Jennifer Peterson. Actually, I didn't think Jennifer was really all that new and different. Maybe she was the same person she used to be before she moved to Canfield—before we all made her too nervous to act like herself.

After she sat down, she glanced over her shoulder at me. I gave her a small, unobtrusive thumbs-up sign. No one around needed to know what I was signaling about; after all, it was Ms. Lombardi's English class and for all anyone knew we were referring to our joint project. Jennifer beamed at me.

Then Allie leaned over toward Jennifer and I heard her whisper, "I love your outfit." I was as glad as if Allie had given me the compliment.

"Good morning!" Ms. Lombardi said as soon as the bell had rung. She glanced around the room to check attendance, pausing a moment as she saw Jennifer. Ms. Lombardi was pretty cool about not embarrassing anyone, but I saw her give Jennifer a warm smile.

At last she closed her attendance book. "Whose project is ready today?"

Jennifer swiveled slightly to catch my eye and I pointed to the back of the room, where our poster was wrapped in brown paper. I'd finished it earlier than I had thought I would.

Before I had a chance to volunteer our team, Liz Barrow and her partner, Nick Melton, volunteered first. They did a Herman Melville story, "Bartleby the Scrivener," but they did it as a dialogue between a Valley Girl and a Surfer Guy. It's a mystery story about this man, Bartleby, who takes a job as a copier, or scrivener. One day he suddenly starts refusing to do anything he's asked to do, and he never says why.

It was really hysterical. Liz would say, "Like, I was wondering if you would, like, mind doing this thing for me, guy?" And Nick would respond, "Well, like, listen, dude, I'm just gonna hang ten, know what I mean?" Then Liz would say "That's a tubular concept but, like, would you please really, like, do it now?" The whole class was laughing by the time they were finished.

"Very innovative," Ms. Lombardi told them, accepting their script. Then she looked right at me. "Rosie, would you and Jennifer mind being next?"

I didn't really mind, except that Liz and Nick were going to be a tough act to follow. But I couldn't really use that as an excuse, so I got the poster from the back of the room and took off the brown wrapper. Jennifer and I walked to the front of the room.

I was a little nervous about displaying our work to the class, but to my surprise Jennifer didn't seem nearly as reluctant. She looked very confident, and that made me feel better about what we were about to unveil. Maybe our partnership worked in more ways than one.

I set the poster on the chalk tray below the blackboard. It was bright and eye-catching. Still, my hands were sweating when I started to describe our work. "We chose 'The Ransom of Red Chief.' Our poster illustrates the story's punchline—the kidnappers being terrorized by their 'victim' as they realize that Red Chief's own father doesn't want him back."

I turned to Jennifer. She said, "I tried to write a funny poem that conveyed the same idea." Then she read her poem aloud. It sounded even better when she read it, I thought, because she knew just how to emphasize the words so that the poem's rhythm worked.

I could see a lot of people smiling while Jennifer was reading, but I was amazed when she finished and people started clapping!

Ms. Lombardi came over to get a closer look at our work. Then she told the class, "This is really very good. Before you leave, everyone should come up here to see it better."

Jennifer and I slid back into our seats, glad our presentation was over. After class, I stopped by Jennifer's desk.

She smiled at me as she finished collecting her books. "We survived."

"Yes, we did. I thought we were dead when the first project was so good!" I confessed.

We sauntered into the hall where my friends were waiting for me. The five of us began walking toward the cafeteria.

"Where did you get those great shoes?" Julie asked.

"I got them at Twinkle Toes in the Pine Tree Mall," Jennifer told her.

"I was in there just last week," Julie said. "I saw plain ballet slippers, but not any with embroidery."

Jennifer looked a little self-conscious. "I did the embroidery myself."

"Wow! I'm impressed," Allie said. "Do you think you could show me how to do it?"

"Sure," Jennifer said shyly.

"I'll save a table for five while you guys get on line," Becky volunteered, piling our books in a huge stack.

I relaxed inwardly. I had been a little worried about what would happen when we got to the cafeteria. I didn't think my friends would expect Jennifer to go sit by herself again, but I was glad Becky had just taken it for granted that Jennifer would sit with us. I think Jennifer was glad, too.

Lunch was okay. I could tell my friends were trying hard to be friendly to Jennifer, but the conversation was strained. We weren't used to eating lunch with anyone else, and no one but me knew Jennifer that well.

The worst part, though, was when I asked Jennifer some stupid question about Bear, like how was he doing or something. Since Julie hadn't been in the park with us that day, she didn't know who—or what—Bear was.

"Bear?" she asked. "Is that your brother's nick-name?"

"Bear's my dog," Jennifer replied. "He's also one of my best friends."

"Sounds like you really like him," Julie commented.

"Dogs are great to have around," Jennifer went on, probably grateful to have something she could talk about. "Especially if you're down or feeling lonely. Sometimes when I felt sad about moving here, Bear would come over and nuzzle me, almost like he was trying to cheer me up. Then, if I still wouldn't smile, he'd go through his tricks—you know, begging, shaking hands, rolling over. Believe me, when you're down in the dumps, a warm, friendly dog is better than a snooty cat."

"My cat, Dizzy, brushes up against me when she knows I'm sad," Julie said flatly.

"Oh," Jennifer said, "I didn't mean . . ."

But it was too late. The bell rang, and Julie took off. Becky and Allie packed up and left as if they were in a big hurry, too.

Jennifer and I slowly got up from the table.

"I didn't mean to insult Julie," Jennifer said miserably.

"I know," I said. "Don't worry, she isn't really mad. She's just . . . she's just a very abrupt person sometimes." It was true—Julie *was* very abrupt. I didn't think that was all it was, though. When you've grown up with a person, you get to know her moods pretty well. And I had a feeling Julie was pretty mad.

"Do you have the list?" Becky asked. It was after school, and Becky, Allie, Julie, and I were walking to the Pine Tree Mall to get supplies for Jennifer's party.

"Right here," I said, waving the list in the air.

Nobody had said anything for the few minutes after we'd left school. Now that Becky had broken the ice, I decided to plunge into the chilly waters.

"Um, Julie?" I began. "You know, Jennifer didn't mean to insult you at lunch today."

"What are you, Jennifer's interpreter?" Julie said. There was no mistaking the sarcasm in her voice.

"No," I said. "But she felt terrible about it. She told me so."

We walked along in silence. When we got to the end of the block, I couldn't stand it anymore.

"Julie," I said, "I could tell you were really angry the way you rushed off at lunch. But it wasn't such a terrible thing to say, and I know Jennifer didn't mean it the way it sounded."

Allie and Becky were in front of Julie and me by now. I could hear them talking softly about a new music video they'd seen.

Julie folded her arms across her chest and kept walking.

"Julie, please don't be angry at Jennifer," I went

on. "Really, it was just a mistake. She didn't mean it."

"You're right, Rosie, I am mad!" Julie practically yelled at me. "But I'm not mad at that stupid dog-face Jennifer! I'm mad at *you!*"

"What did I do?" I was completely bewildered.

"I left lunch in a hurry because I had to get to class," Julie continued. "Sure, Jennifer made a stupid remark, but what do I care? What bothers me is that my best friend has suddenly turned into a dog lover! I feel like you're not my friend anymore, Rosie, because you're too busy being Jennifer's!"

"Julie . . ." I didn't know what to say. I knew it seemed that way, but it wasn't true. Since Julie had been so busy lately, we hadn't been spending as much time together as we usually did. I'd been feeling a little left out of Julie's life, too.

If Julie had only known what I'd been doing! The day before, after the Party Line meeting, Becky, Allie, and I had met at Allie's house to go over plans for Julie's surprise party. We'd wrapped all her presents with special lacy decorations on top. We'd made up a shopping list for the dinner, and each of us had agreed to buy some of the ingredients. I'd been working really hard on designing a special card for Julie. And Becky, Allie, and I were going shopping later in the week to buy special party decorations. It wasn't fair for Julie to say I wasn't her friend anymore.

"Julie, that's just not true!" I finally said. "You're

my best friend in the whole world. No one could replace you!"

Allie and Becky had stopped pretending to ignore us by now, and they were both looking at Julie and me.

"Julie," Allie said, "If you knew—" I hoped Allie wasn't going to give away all our secret plans. She stopped and looked at me. "If you knew all the nice things Rosie says about you all the time, you'd never think that."

"That's true," Becky said. "Come on, guys. Please don't fight."

Julie looked at each of us. Finally she smiled. It was a very tiny smile, but a smile nevertheless.

"I'm sorry," she said. "I've just been feeling so out of it lately, because I hardly ever see you guys."

"Well, I haven't seen much of you lately, either," I told her.

"Yeah, so let's not spoil everything by fighting, okay?" Becky said.

I heaved a big sigh of relief. It seemed as if the fight was over.

When we got to The Perfect Party, our first stop was the rack of party invitations. I wanted to pick out something nice for Jennifer, and I was looking through some flowery invitations in one section. My friends were all behind me, looking through a different section.

All of a sudden I heard Allie start giggling. Becky said, "Oh, this is perfect!" When I turned around, they were all laughing and pointing at a package of invitations.

"The picture even *looks* like Jennifer!" Julie snickered.

When I leaned over to see what was so funny, I felt like bursting into tears. The invitations had "Have a *barking* good time!" printed across the top. Underneath was a picture of a big, laughing dog. I didn't want to say anything that would start another fight, and I didn't want to seem like a goody-two-shoes, either. One thing was for sure: I couldn't let my friends see how upset I was.

"Very funny," I said. Then I decided to pretend they were serious, so they would think I was going along with the joke. "It's a great picture, but Jennifer's hair is longer than that," I said. "And don't you think the design is a little childish for a thirteenth-birthday party?"

It worked. Allie stuck the invitations back where they'd found them. "Let's see what you've got, Rosie," she said.

I handed her one package with a pretty garden scene, and one that had a bold design of ribbons and bows.

"I can't decide. You pick."

Allie put the flowery one into our shopping basket.

We went through the rest of the store quickly, and in twenty minutes we were standing at the cash register. I had mixed feelings about the afternoon spent with my friends, but I felt good about the things we had bought. Jennifer's 'Welcome to Canfield' party was going to be pretty special—almost as special as Julie's sleepover surprise party.

Nine

Before I knew it, the week was over. We'd addressed the invitations to Jennifer's party and had handed them out to all the girls in our class. By Friday, most had said they'd come to the party.

The upcoming weekend was going to be pretty busy. It was the last chunk of time I'd have to get things done before Julie's and Jennifer's parties.

Fortunately, Julie was busy on Saturday, so the conspiracy—as Becky, Allie, and I had started calling ourselves—was having another secret meeting at my house.

"Checklist," Becky said, and held out her hand like a surgeon waiting for a scalpel.

"Checklist," Allie confirmed, handing it to her.

"Dinner supplies," Becky announced.

We had just finished unpacking our grocery bags and had put everything in a special corner of the refrigerator. We'd made certain we had enough of everything we needed, because we were going to be too busy with homework and Jennifer's party preparations to do much shopping later in the week.

"Check," I said.

"Presents," Becky said next.

"Double-check," Allie said, pointing to the small pile of fancy packages we were going to hide in the sideboard in the dining room.

"Card," Becky called off.

"I hope you guys like this," I said as I pulled the card I'd worked on for so long out of its envelope.

"Rosie, it looks terrific," Becky said, forgetting that she was trying to imitate a drill sergeant.

"Oh, Rosie, it does," Allie agreed. "You could probably sell this design to a card company and make a lot of money."

I was glad my friends liked my artwork. I'd used pastels for the cover, which was a picture of a girl who looked a lot like Julie wearing a beautiful pink party dress just like the one Goldie had sent her. She was dancing with a really cute guy (who looked a tiny bit like Mark Harris) dressed in a black tuxedo. To make it look as though the couple was whirling around a ballroom, I'd drawn tall columns in the background and made Julie's dress swing out from her legs.

I'd carefully written across the top, "Congratulations! You may be growing up. . . ." When you opened the card you saw the rest of the inscription: "But you're not going anywhere without *us*!

There was a drawing on the inside, too. It showed all four of us—me, Julie, Becky, and Allie—leaping into the air, like in that car commercial.

"You really like it?" I asked.

"I love it!" Allie answered.

"Me, too," Becky chimed in.

"I guess we should fill it out now," I said. "It will be one less thing to do next Friday."

I passed around a purple felt-tip pen. Purple is Julie's favorite color. We each wrote something funny in the card and signed our names. Carefully, I put the card back in the special envelope I'd made for it—out of purple paper, of course!

"What else should we do?" Becky asked.

"You ordered the cake, right?" I asked her. The Party Line orders all its cakes from Matthew, the baker who makes the desserts for the Moondance Café. That way we get a good discount. Even though Julie's surprise wasn't an official Party Line party, it was probably the most important party we'd thrown yet. And, after all, what's a party without cake?

"Yes, I'll bring it with me Friday afternoon when I come over." We were all meeting at my house right after school on Friday to start dinner preparations.

I didn't know how we could possibly keep everything straight. The next day we'd be going over our plans for Jennifer's party at the weekly Party Line meeting in Becky's attic.

"So what's left?" asked Allie. "I keep having this awful thought that we'll suddenly discover we've forgotten something next Friday just as Julie's coming up the front steps."

"Don't even think such a thing!" I said.

"Yeah, quit being such a worrywart, Allie," Becky said. "I mean, I know you can't help it, but . . ."

Allie put her hands on her hips and tried to give Becky a steely look. Of course she started laughing and ruined her act.

"No, really," I said, "I think we've got everything under control. I'm going to set the table after school on Friday, before you guys get here. My mom said we can use all the good stuff: china, crystal, silverware, linen napkins, and tablecloth. And—ta-da!" With a flourish I produced four tall purple candles.

"Rosie, that's great of you to remember the candles," Allie said admiringly.

"You have candlesticks, right?" Becky asked.

"Yes, and they're very fancy," I said. They were cut crystal that had been in my mother's family for nearly a hundred years. My mom had said we could use them if we were careful. I was planning to be *very* careful.

Becky looked at the checklist one last time.

"You've got everything set with Mrs. Berger?" she asked.

"Yes," I said. "Heather is going to bring Julie's sleepover stuff here right after school on Friday, and Mrs. Berger is going to keep Julie busy until just before she brings her over."

"Great!" Allie said. "It would be awful if Julie decided to come over early or something."

"Does Julie know about it yet?" Becky wanted to

know. "I mean, does she know she's coming over to watch a movie?"

I wrinkled my nose. "No. If I ask Julie this far ahead of time, she'll know something's up. But I'm renting her favorite movie, and her mom is going to make sure she doesn't have anything else to do that night. I'll ask her Thursday, and I know she'll say yes. Julie's going to be so busy this week that she'll be dying to get away and take a break!"

"This official meeting of the Party Line will now come to order!" Becky announced.

I'd been wondering what Julie was hiding behind her back, and now I found out. She brought out a little gavel and banged sharply on the floor with it. "Order in the court!" she cried.

Julie was always trying to come up with new ways to tease Becky about her presidential manner. This was the best yet.

Becky slitted her eyes until they were practically closed. "Bread and water for thirty days for disturbing the peace," she sentenced Julie.

"Fat chance," Julie crowed as she ripped open a gigantic bag of sour cream- and chive-flavored potato chips.

"I take it back," Becky said."As long as you give me first shot at those potato chips."

"Deal," Julie said, tossing her the bag.

"If you guys have finished the comedy routine," Allie said, "maybe we can really get started. I have

to visit my grandmother later, so I can't stay long."
Allie's grandmother lived in the Pine Villa retire-
ment complex nearby, and Allie went over there a
couple of times a week, often to run errands for her
grandmother. Becky went with her a lot—so much
that she'd even been "adopted" as a grandchild by
two people at Pine Villa.

"There isn't much to go over, really," I said. "We
have most of the supplies, don't we?"

"I ordered the cake," Becky put in.

"I've got the Canfield Middle School sweatshirt,"
Allie said next.

"And I bought party favors," said Julie, bringing
out her last surprise.

"Julie, that's great!" I said. "I thought we'd have
to schedule another shopping trip after school some
day this week."

"Well, I was at the mall anyway, and this stuff
didn't cost that much," Julie said.

"So we have everything, then?" Becky said.

"We'll need to get snacks and soda sometime before Saturday," Allie said, checking her organization sheet.

"Otherwise, we have everything except the final
guest list," Becky said.

"Only two people haven't RSVPed yet," I said.
"Melissa Burke and Gina DeSantis."

"I'll find out if they're coming," Julie volunteered.
"I'll call them later tonight and let you know. I did

buy favors for them—we can always give them to Jennifer if Melissa and Gina don't come."

"I can't believe we've gotten everything organized so quickly," Becky said. "This must be a Party Line record. As far as the planning goes, Jennifer's party is a success already."

Becky and Julie got up to pick out some music. Julie would be putting together a music tape for Jennifer's party, but right then they were looking for something we felt like hearing at the moment. Allie was making notes on her organization sheet.

All the talk about Jennifer's party had been making me feel guilty. I hadn't spoken much with her in the past week. I'd been really busy and whenever I was free, I just never ran into her. I noticed she hadn't been sitting by herself in the lunchroom, but she hadn't sat with us since that first time.

I hated to admit it, but I hadn't exactly gone out of my way to spend any time with Jennifer. After the fight with Julie, I didn't want to do anything that might make my friends mad at me.

I felt like a rat. I worried that if I acted friendly to Jennifer my friends wouldn't like it. But I also worried that Jennifer would think I was two-faced for ignoring her. *And if she thought that,* I thought miserably, *she'd probably be right.*

I promised myself I'd call Jennifer as soon as I got home. Actually, she had called me once during the week about a homework assignment, but I'd had to get off the phone quickly because Julie had stopped by. Remembering that, I felt even worse.

Thump! A pillow bounced off my nose and fell in my lap.

"Whatever you're thinking about, it must be pretty serious," Julie said. "Did you even notice we put on your favorite Bastille song?"

I smiled at my best friend. "Sorry," I said. "I was thinking about everything I have to get done this week."

"Like what?" Julie said. "Everything's taken care of."

That's what you think! I thought to myself. *Julie Berger, you are in for a big surprise Friday night!* Out loud I said, "I was thinking about homework and stuff."

"This girl needs help," Julie called to Becky and Allie. "It's still the weekend and she's thinking about school already."

Becky turned up the music and Allie tossed me the bag of chips.

"Rosie, you need to lighten up and party," Julie told me.

If only everything were that easy!

Ten

I did call Jennifer when I got home that Sunday, and told her I was sorry I'd been so busy during the week. It turned out we both have subscriptions to *Saucy* magazine, and we talked about some of the clothes in the newest issue.

"Speaking of clothes," Jennifer said, "what do you think I should wear on Saturday?"

"What about your rainbow sweater and your jean skirt with those red cowboy boots?" I suggested. The rainbow sweater was another of Jennifer's grandmother's originals; it didn't exactly have a rainbow on it, but it did have about a million colors in a bold, abstract pattern. It was actually brighter than a rainbow.

"Rosie, that's brilliant!" Jennifer said. "I never would have put those things together. You're a real friend!"

It felt good when Jennifer told me that. I just wished I could live up to it.

* * *

Monday we did our party shopping after school. We bought soda and lots of great snacks, like cheese curls, corn chips, and cheese-flavored popcorn. Becky agreed to store it all at her house until Saturday, so we were set.

It was a good thing we did everything early in the week, too, because Ms. Pernell sprang a surprise biology test on us. The test was on Friday, so none of us did much besides study right up until then.

At the end of the day on Friday we burst out of school as if we'd been fired from a cannon. I raced home to get the dining room table set.

By four o'clock, Becky and Allie were sitting in the kitchen with me, poring over recipes and lining up ingredients. We spent about an hour getting everything ready. Julie was coming over around six o'clock, so we had a half-hour to clean up before we actually started cooking.

Allie and I straightened up and put things in the dishwasher while Becky arranged a ton of fabulous ingredients on two pizza rounds. Those were going to stay in the refrigerator until after dinner, when we'd heat them up to eat while we watched the movie.

I'd wanted to rent *Summer in Paris*, but Julie hated mushy romance movies like that. Because it was her special night, I'd splurged on *Deadly Target*. It was an action movie about two cops, and it had a lot of comedy in it, too. It had been a big hit and had just came out in the video stores the week before.

I'd had to go to the store three weeks earlier just to reserve it for that night.

At six o'clock, the chicken was in the oven and the vegetables and the rice were almost ready. I heard a car pull up outside, and I ran quickly to light the candles on the dining room table.

My mom let Julie in, and Julie started up the stairs. I heard her say, "Hey, Rosie?"

"I'm in the dining room," I called. Julie thumped back downstairs.

"What are you doing in here?" she asked as she came in. When she saw the candles and the table set for company, she whistled. "It looks great in here. Are your parents having company?"

"No, I am," I said, smiling.

"You're kidding!" Julie exclaimed. "Like who?"

"Like you!" Becky and Allie bounced in from the kitchen and joined me.

The look on Julie's face was incredible.

"You guys did this for me?" she squealed. "I can't believe it!"

I showed her where to sit—at the head of the table, of course. Becky and Allie bustled about, setting out salads at each plate and bringing out the dinner rolls.

"This is the best," Julie said. The soft candlelight gleamed off the silverware and the gilt edges of the china. Julie's eyes glowed with happiness.

"I know it sounds stupid, but I just can't believe

you guys did all this for me," she said. "It almost makes me feel like crying."

"No mush!" Becky hollered. "Julie Berger, don't you dare get all misty-eyed on us."

"I'm actually kind of insulted," I kidded.

"Why?" Allie looked at me, wide-eyed. She was probably worried that Julie and I were going to start fighting again.

"Well, Julie thinks this is all we're doing for her," I teased. "She doesn't give us credit for thinking big, I guess."

Julie perked up immediately. "There's more?"

"Wait and see," Becky told her.

While we crunched salad, we answered all of Julie's questions.

"How did you guys plan all this behind my back?" she wanted to know.

"It wasn't easy," Allie sighed. "I almost gave it away twice, but luckily you were being kind of dense."

"Your mom and Heather helped, too," I added.

"Heather?" Julie was shocked. "What did she do?"

"You'll see when the time comes," Becky said mysteriously.

The timer pinged in the kitchen just as we were finished.

"Perfect timing." Becky smiled as she stood up.

"Just stay right where you are," I commanded Julie.

When Allie, Becky, and I paraded in from the

kitchen with the main course, Julie's mouth actually fell open. We had arranged everything in pretty serving trays.

First I placed the chicken Kiev on everyone's dinner plate, starting with Julie. Allie followed right behind me, ladling scoops of rice pilaf off to one side. Lastly, Becky spooned my green beans almondine onto the plates. Since Becky's parents run the best restaurant in Canfield, she was very particular about presentation, the way the food was arranged on the plate. The green beans provided a bright slash of color that made the meal look even more appetizing.

Julie has a legendary appetite. Naturally, she had seconds of everything—although how any of us managed to eat when we were talking a mile a minute is truly amazing.

When dinner was finished, it was about seven o'clock. That was the moment we'd been waiting for: time for the cake and the presents.

We still weren't letting Julie do any work. When the table was cleared, Becky brought out dessert plates while Allie rummaged in the sideboard for our gifts. I laid the card on Julie's plate and left the room.

When I returned with the cake—triple chocolate cream, Julie's favorite—it was time to open the presents. That's when I realized how touched Julie was by our surprise party. Usually she just ripped the wrapping off any which way, but that night she carefully removed each lacy bow and put them off to the side before she neatly removed the wrapping paper.

When she opened the card, I thought she'd get all misty-eyed again, but she managed to fight back her tears. She swore she would keep the card forever.

She loved her small presents, and especially our explanation of how and why we'd chosen them for her. The perfume was a big hit, but an even bigger hit was the story of how we'd been so excited about getting it that Allie had actually walked right into Dylan Matthews.

"He really is cute," Julie said encouragingly.

"Isn't he?" Allie said.

Julie raised her eyebrows at me across the table as if to say, "You're darn right I'm not the only one growing up." Then Becky shoved the biggest box, the one with the nightgown, into her lap.

"Another present?" Julie yelled. When she opened the box, she nearly screamed with delight. "This is the most beautiful nightgown I've ever had," she said. And then she really did start crying.

"I feel like such a dope," she sniffled, "but you guys are the greatest." Becky always acted like she thought this kind of behavior was hopelessly babyish, but I noticed that as she flounced out to get a box of tissues her eyes were glistening, too.

We were just getting started on the cake when the doorbell rang. We weren't expecting anyone, so I was surprised.

I was even more surprised when I opened the door and saw Jennifer standing on the doorstep.

"How did you get here?" It was kind of late to be bicycling and, anyway, I didn't see a bike anywhere. Besides, I could've sworn that I had heard a car pull away as I opened the door.

"My brother dropped me off," Jennifer said.

"Your brother?" I nearly shrieked. I knew her brother was only seven years old.

"My *older* brother," Jennifer added quickly.

This was getting too complicated for me to sort out. Since when did she have two brothers? But one thing was pretty clear: I was going to have to invite Jennifer in.

I could hear my mom come into the hall behind me. "Who is it, Rosie?" she asked. "Oh, hi, Jennifer," she said warmly when she peeked around the door. "Rosie, invite your friend in."

That settled it. "Come on in," I said, trying not to sound as reluctant as I felt.

I brought Jennifer into the dining room. My friends looked as stunned as I'd been a minute earlier. But the shock on their faces was nothing compared to Jennifer's.

"I didn't realize you . . . oh, I'm sorry," she stammered. She looked so anguished that Becky leaped up from the table.

"I'll get another chair," she said. Allie took another dessert dish out of the breakfront, and I sliced a piece of cake.

"Really," Jennifer said, "I just stopped by for a minute."

"Jennifer, we're inviting you to join us," Becky said. "I hope you're not going to insult us by refusing to sit down."

Jennifer flashed me a look of pure alarm. She didn't know Becky well enough to realize she was kidding. Especially after our disastrous lunch with her, I knew Jennifer was afraid to say the wrong thing. Fortunately, Becky gave her a big grin.

"Please?" Becky said, smiling.

"Thanks," Jennifer said and slid into the chair. "What am I interrupting?" she asked. I thought that was pretty brave of her.

"Julie is going to have her bat mitzvah in one week," I said.

Before I could begin to explain what that was, Jennifer smiled and said, *"Mazel tov."*

"Thanks," Julie said, beaming at her.

"*What* did you say?" Allie asked.

"My best friend in Minnesota had a bat mitzvah ceremony before I moved," Jennifer explained. "*Mazel tov* means 'best wishes' or 'congratulations.' When Beth was bat mitzvahed, I remember we said that to her."

"Well, if you know all about it," Becky said, "we should probably explain that we decided to throw Julie a surprise party to get her in the mood for the big celebration next week."

"And since her bat mitzvah means she's officially coming of age—" I went on.

"Our party theme is 'Now You're a Woman,' " Allie finished.

"That's neat," Jennifer said. "You got presents and everything!" She could see the boxes and crumpled wrapping paper at Julie's end of the table.

"Why did you come over?" I finally asked. I didn't want to be rude. I was just very curious.

"Well . . ." Jennifer seemed embarrassed. "My mom was going to drop off an envelope for you for the . . . you know, the party tomorrow. And I thought maybe you could show me how to wear those fake nails you use." She blushed a little. "I wanted to do something special for tomorrow. My brother was going out anyway, and he said he'd drop me off.

"I feel terrible," she went on. "I thought you could help me with the nails, and then I'd call my mom to pick me up. I didn't know you were having a private party." Jennifer kept her eyes on the table the entire time she was talking. Then she rummaged around in a shoulder bag she'd brought in with her and handed me an envelope. "This is from my mom."

It was an awkward moment, but Becky saved us by saying, "Try the cake. It's really good."

"I don't get it," I said as we ate. "I didn't know you had an older brother."

"He's been away at college," Jennifer explained.

"You have a brother in college?" Julie asked.

Leave it to Julie to focus immediately on the boy angle.

I was so glad my friends were being nice to Jennifer. And once she got over her initial discomfort at having interrupted us, Jennifer seemed to relax and have a good time.

Julie showed Jennifer her presents, with Becky and Allie keeping up a running commentary of explanations. When the cake was gone, I had a decision to make. I got up to start clearing the table, and Allie and Becky immediately jumped up to help me.

Julie, of course, wasn't allowed to do any work, and I told Jennifer to stay where she was, too. "You're our guest, too," I told her.

I felt a little guilty deserting Julie, but I figured she could handle a few minutes by herself with Jennifer.

Once the three of us were in the kitchen, though, we put the plates down and huddled.

"What should we do?" I whispered.

"I guess we should invite Jennifer to stay," Allie said. I was glad she'd said it first.

"She'll have to call her mother, anyway," Becky said. "She might not want to stay."

"But what if she does? Would you guys mind?" I asked.

"I think she's nice," Allie said decisively. "And I

think you're right, Rosie. We should give her a chance."

"She's been fine so far," Becky agreed. "Why not? We have to give her a party tomorrow anyway, so we may as well get to know her better. At least she came after dinner was over," Becky added.

"Do you think Julie will mind?"

"Did you see the way her eyes lit up when she found out Jennifer has a brother in college?" Becky asked, giving me a look.

"She's right," Allie giggled. "I don't think Julie will mind."

We had been gone only about two minutes, but when we came back to the dining room, Julie and Jennifer were talking a mile a minute. About boys, of course.

"We have another surprise for you, Julie," I said. "And, Jennifer, we have to ask you something. Will you both come into the den?"

Julie looked pleased; she knew the surprise was another special treat. Jennifer looked bewildered.

When we all got to the den, Julie saw the sleeping bags spread out on the floor.

"It's a sleepover!" she shouted gleefully. "How did you get my stuff here?"

"That's where Heather came in," Becky explained.

"Jennifer," Allie said, "we were wondering if you

could call your mother and see if you could spend the night, too. That is, if you want to," she added.

Jennifer looked unsure of what to do. I could tell she wanted to stay, but I think she was worried about butting in where she didn't belong.

"Please say yes," Julie said.

"It'll be fun," Becky added.

Jennifer looked at me. "There's plenty of room," I told her. "If you want, you could borrow some of my pajamas."

"We could pile up quilts if you don't have a sleeping bag," Allie suggested.

"I give in," Jennifer said, laughing. "If you're sure it's okay with you, I'll call my mom."

Julie pointed to the phone in the corner.

Jennifer's mother said it was fine for her to sleep over, and she showed up about fifteen minutes later with a small duffle bag and a sleeping bag.

We ended up having a great time.

First we watched the movie, which was great. We had an intermission in the middle of it, and Becky made cheese-flavored popcorn.

Around eleven o'clock we put on our pajamas. We teased Julie about her new nightgown until she agreed to try it on for us. It looked great on her.

"Wait until Mark sees it," I teased, pulling out my camera.

"Rosie! Don't you dare!" Julie yanked a blanket up off the floor and hid inside it.

"I was only kidding, Julie," I said.

Julie decided that since she was going to be lying around on the floor eating pizza it might be better if she didn't wear her new nightgown just yet. With a sigh, she changed into her regular pajamas.

We didn't stay up too late, but it was still hard to get up the next morning. My mom had bought a big box of danish and we sat around the kitchen table, a little bleary-eyed, for nearly an hour after we got up. We needed that much time to wake up fully.

It was about eleven o'clock when Becky and Allie decided to walk home. The plan was that we'd all meet at Jennifer's house around one; the party was at two. Julie's mother came to pick her up not long afterward, and they gave Jennifer a ride home.

As I shut the front door behind them, I smiled to myself. It's funny how things have a way of turning out for the best. I was glad that Jennifer had gotten to know—and like—my best friends a lot better last night. And I was especially glad that they had gotten along well with her, too.

Maybe the "Welcome to Canfield" party would be our best party ever.

Eleven

"What do think of your party?" I whispered to Jennifer.

"It's the best," she said, her eyes shining.

Because this was for kids our age, we didn't organize it like our usual kiddie parties. The party was in the Petersons' family room, which was even cooler than their living room. It was a big room built onto the back of the house, and it had lots of windows.

We had arranged big bowls of snack foods around the room, and we'd given each guest her gaily wrapped party favors as soon as she came in. Everyone had immediately tied on their friendship bracelets, and everyone was wearing their green Canfield sweatshirts, even Jennifer. As soon as we'd given it to her, she'd put it on. It looked cute with her jean skirt and her red boots. (I hadn't forgotten to help her with the fake nails, either, even though we hadn't gotten around to them the night before. We'd put them on right before the party guests arrived.)

We'd decided on a lot of fun party games, but the

first order of the day was the party theme. The first game was for everyone—except Jennifer, of course— to tell their favorite story about something funny that had happened to them in school. The idea of this game was to help Jennifer get to know everyone a little better—and to have fun.

I went first. "Jennifer, you cannot turn thirteen in Canfield without knowing a few important things about your new classmates."

"Can I take notes?" Jennifer asked, grinning wickedly.

Julie's hand flew to her heart as if the suggestion was scandalous. "Never! You'll be learning secrets none of us want to see in print."

I told the story about my first art project in third grade. I'd made my homeroom teacher, Ms. Costello, a clay mug for Christmas. But I hadn't known that it is necessary to fire clay in a kiln. Once the mug dried, I had thought it was done because it felt hard enough to me. I'd painted the outside with bright enamel paints, and Ms. Costello had seemed really happy when I gave it to her.

In fact, she'd used it for hot chocolate the day of our class Christmas party. But because I had never baked the clay, it couldn't stand up to all the hot liquid being poured into it.

"It melted all over Ms. Costello's desk!" Becky said, laughing.

"Oh, how awful!" Jennifer exclaimed.

"You bet it was awful! The hot chocolate went

all over the place and the mug just sort of imploded into the desk. It took the janitor twenty minutes to scrape it off with a knife," Allie said, giggling.

"What about the time Liz led the pledge of allegiance?" Gina DeSantis reminded us.

"Give me a break!" Liz Barrow said. "I was in first grade!"

"Come on, tell!"

"I never really understood what the words were," Liz shrugged. "I thought I knew them, though. So when our first grade teacher said she'd let a different kid lead the pledge every day, I waved my hand so frantically she picked me first."

"And this is what Liz said," Melissa Burke picked up the story. " 'I led the pigeons to the flag of the united stairs of America. . . .' "

" 'And the tooth fairy public of which it stands,' " Julie finished. "It was so hysterical!"

"The whole class was cracking up, and there I was, standing up front as proud as can be," Liz said ruefully. "I had no idea how wrong my version of the pledge was."

Everyone went through their stories, and it was really funny. Jennifer even volunteered to tell about one of her most mortifying moments, when she was standing in assembly and the elastic in her slip gave out.

"My slip was in a heap at my feet," Jennifer said. "I couldn't figure out how to pick it up and stuff it in my bookbag without anyone seeing."

"So what did you do?" Liz asked.

"I just left it there," Jennifer said, and everyone cracked up.

"Can you imagine what the janitor must have thought when he was cleaning up later and found it?" Cathy Frey howled.

"That's the worst part, actually," Jennifer admitted. "My teacher found it after we'd filed out. She held it up in front of the whole class and said, 'Someone left this in the auditorium. Please come get it.'"

"Oh, no," Allie breathed.

"I thought I'd never live it down," Jennifer said.

By the time we'd finished, everyone was getting along like old friends. We took a break between games. Julie had put together a terrific party tape, and we bopped around the room laying waste to six kinds of potato chips (regular, barbecue, sour cream and chive, crinkle-cut, hot and spicy, and sweet potato) and every other kind of snack food you can think of.

The next game we played was Guess Who. It goes like this: The first person thinks of another person in the room and everyone tries to guess who it is by asking questions like, "If she were a car, what kind of car would she be?" Then it just goes around the room. Some of the questions are pretty funny, but once you know who the person is, the answers are even funnier. But the main reason we picked it for the party was that it's another good way to get to know people better.

We found out that Liz thought that if Julie were an animal, she'd be a flamingo. And that Becky thought that if Jennifer were a plant, she'd be a sunflower. Jennifer thought Cathy would be tomato sauce if she were a food, which was actually pretty clever. (Cathy Frey is one of the bounciest, liveliest people I know, and she has the same kind of zip and zest as a good sauce. She's the sort of person who always makes things more fun just by showing up.) When it turned out that Melissa thought Allie would make a great filing cabinet, everyone thought it was hilarious except Allie, who was genuinely bewildered.

"Me? A filing cabinet?" she asked.

"What else for Miss Organization?" Becky retorted.

"Or Miss I-Always-Know-the-Answer-in-Class?" Liz countered.

"Really, Allie, it's a compliment," Jennifer told her. Allie finally accepted that, but she didn't look convinced.

Around four o'clock we brought out the birthday cake, a peach upside-down cake. Mrs. Peterson had said it was one of Jennifer's favorites. It turned out to be really good, too. The only thing we didn't like about it was that it was a little tricky planting the birthday candles in the peach slices that covered the top of the cake, but Becky figured out how to do it by making little holes with a sharp toothpick first.

Instead of icing, we had placed a circle of gold foil

in the center of the cake. Silver glitter spelled out "Happy Birthday" and "Welcome to Canfield, Jennifer." I had made it myself with gold paper and my handy glitter gun. With the candles glinting off it, it really looked spectacular.

After the cake, Jennifer opened her presents. She got a lot of nice stuff—pretty stationery, a beautiful blue silky scarf that matched her eyes (that was from Allie), a Bastille cassette that I knew she didn't have from me, wild knee socks, stuff like that. But of all the great stuff she got, one of the biggest hits was a black Ben & Jerry's sweatshirt from Becky.

"So you can get into the spirit of living in Vermont," Becky said as Jennifer opened it. "Also, I thought black would really show off your blond hair."

"I love it," Jennifer said. And when Allie shyly walked over and pinned a green and white "I ♥ Canfield" button to the front of the sweatshirt, I thought Jennifer might even start crying.

After all the presents had been opened and all the cake had been eaten, Julie raised her glass of soda and said, "A toast! A toast!" Everyone quieted down and looked expectantly at her.

"To Jennifer: Happy Birthday, and happy days in your new hometown!"

There was a second toast after that. Jennifer held up her glass and said, "To new friends and new beginnings."

As everyone laughed and cheered, I had to marvel

to myself. The girl who'd sat by herself at lunch had come a long way. And The Party Line had helped a lot.

That was probably our best party ever. We'd had fun, earned money, and really helped someone, too. What more can a person ask?

Special Party Tip
Rosie's Icebreakers

An icebreaker isn't a little hammer you use to smash ice cubes. It's something designed to get people having fun at a party.

Games are a great way to get people talking, and you can have a lot of fun playing them, too. Guess Who is described in Chapter 11. Here are some other good games to get the action rolling.

Charades: The object is for someone in the group to correctly identify a word or phrase that is acted out by the person leading the charade. First, everyone in the group agrees on a topic for the charades. You can do song or movie titles, familiar sayings—whatever sounds like the most fun. Then, one at a time, each person gets up and acts out the word or phrase without speaking. For instance, if the word you were trying to get the group to guess was *ball*, you might go about it this way: First you would cup your hand to your ear to indicate that the word sounds like something you're about to act out. As soon as someone in the group figured that out, you would nod and move on to the next part of the charade. You could fall in a heap on the floor and keep doing it until someone guessed *fall*. Then you might imitate a bee—by buzzing or pretending to sting someone—and your audience would have to put together *b* and *fall* to get the word *ball*. And so on until someone correctly guesses the whole thing.

Telephone: Everyone in the group sits in a circle, and one person starts by whispering something to the person next to her. That person repeats it to the next person, and so on and so on until you get to the last person. She says out loud what she heard from the person next to her. Then the person who started the message says out loud what she originally whispered. You'll be surprised at how much a sentence can change as it's repeated from one person to another. By the time it gets to the last person in the group it usually makes no sense whatsoever—and has nothing to do with its original content.